TELL ME TO LIE

CHARLOTTE BYRD

CHARLOTTE BYRD
dangerously addictive

Identifiers

ISBN (e-book): 978-1-63225-059-9

ISBN (paperback): 978-1-63225-060-5

ISBN (hardcover):978-1-63225-061-2

❀ Created with Vellum

There was a time when my debt was the only link we had.

There was a time when I couldn't tell him how much I loved him and he couldn't tell me. There was a time when I thought I could never have enough money.

Now, everything is different.

Nicholas Crawford is a stranger who is becoming more strange with every moment.

I used to think I could make a life with him, but now I'm not so sure.

We have been through too much.

But then he takes a step closer.

Then he whispers something into my ear.

Then presses his lips to my mouth.

Suddenly, everything that was wrong starts to feel so right...

Read the EPIC Conclusion to the addictive TELL ME series by bestselling author Charlotte Byrd.

PRAISE FOR CHARLOTTE BYRD

"Extremely captivating, sexy, steamy, intriguing, and intense!" ★★★★★

"Addictive and impossible to put down." ★★★★★

"I can't get enough of the turmoil, lust, love, drama, and secrets!" ★★★★★

"Fast-paced romantic suspense filled with twists and turns, danger, betrayal, and so much more." ★★★★★

"Decadent, delicious, & dangerously addictive!" - Amazon Review ★★★★★

"Titillation so masterfully woven, no reader can resist its pull. A MUST-BUY!" - Bobbi Koe, Amazon Review ★★★★★

"Captivating!" - Crystal Jones, Amazon Review ★★★★★

"Sexy, secretive, pulsating chemistry..." - Mrs. K, Amazon Reviewer ★★★★★

"Charlotte Byrd is a brilliant writer. I've read loads and I've laughed and cried. She writes a balanced book with brilliant characters. Well done!" -Amazon Review ★★★★★

"Hot, steamy, and a great storyline." - Christine Reese ★★★★★

"My oh my....Charlotte has made me a fan for life." - JJ, Amazon Reviewer ★★★★★

"Wow. Just wow. Charlotte Byrd leaves me speechless and humble... It definitely kept me on the edge of my seat. Once you pick it up, you won't put it down." - Amazon Review ★★★★★

" Intrigue, lust, and great characters...what more could you ask for?!" - Dragonfly Lady ★★★★★

DON'T MISS OUT!

Want to be the first to know about my upcoming sales, new releases and exclusive giveaways?

Bonus Points: Follow me on BookBub and Goodreads!

ALSO BY CHARLOTTE BYRD

All books are available at ALL major retailers! If you can't find it, please email me at charlotte@charlotte-byrd.com

Wedlocked Trilogy
Dangerous Engagement
Lethal Wedding
Fatal Wedding

Tell me Series
Tell Me to Stop
Tell Me to Go
Tell Me to Stay
Tell Me to Run
Tell Me to Fight

Tell Me to Lie

Tangled Series
Tangled up in Ice
Tangled up in Pain
Tangled up in Lace
Tangled up in Hate
Tangled up in Love

Black Series
Black Edge
Black Rules
Black Bounds
Black Contract
Black Limit

Lavish Trilogy
Lavish Lies
Lavish Betrayal
Lavish Obsession

Standalone Novels
Debt
Offer
Unknown
Dressing Mr. Dalton

1

NICHOLAS

WHEN THEY ARREST ME...

The handcuffs are tight around my wrists but the pain doesn't come close to the pain that's surging through my heart. It's as if Olive stuck an ice pick right through it, splintering it into a million little pieces.

I try to breathe but topple over in pain. The seat in the back of the cop car is vinyl and it feels cool against my body. I look out of the window.

The FBI agents and the local police officers are swarming around my recreational vehicle. I force myself to take another deep breath and search through them for Olive.

Where is she?

Where did they take her?

If only I could get a glimpse of her, then I'd know for sure if she had betrayed me.

Or will I?

They are only here because of her. It was she who has turned me in. It was she who led them here.

At first, I had my doubts about her. I wondered if I should trust her.

I had betrayed her, so what would make me think that she wouldn't betray me as well? Still, after talking to her on the phone, I got the sense that she believed me.

I run over every word that we said to each other, first on the phone and then in person. I look for clues that she might have been lying, but nothing comes to mind.

It was so nice to reconnect with her. It was so wonderful to hold her in my arms again. I had missed her so much, maybe I had just convinced myself that she was telling the truth.

I close my eyes and imagine my lips on hers.

Her mouth is soft and inviting and

everything that she has always been. Was it all a lie? Was our whole relationship nothing but fiction or was it only a lie at the end?

Was this her way of showing me how much I had betrayed her?

It starts to snow.

Big thick flakes fall from the sky. Somebody brings me my coat and boots from the RV. Someone else helps me put them on. Three cops crowd around me as they carefully unlock my wrists, fearing that I'm going to make a run for it.

But I won't. It would be a suicide mission.

They want to arrest me but they are willing to shoot me.

I may have committed other crimes, but I never killed anyone, let alone my partner or my ex-girlfriend. And I'll be damned if I let them say that I did, let alone kill me for it.

I may not have much strength now, but I will fight them on this. They will not ruin my name and dirty it up with lies about murder. I never killed anyone and I will not let them put me away for crimes that I didn't commit.

A cop starts the car and we slowly pull

out onto the gravel road. Snow starts to fall faster and faster and the wipers work hard to keep the windshield clean.

Snowplows typically don't come down this far into the woods and I wonder if the rest of the police force crowding around my RV will get out before the majority of the blizzard sweeps in.

I sit back against the seat and look at the snowflakes dance outside the window. I've never been in jail or prison but I've heard the stories about lack of outside time.

Will this be the last time that I see the sky?

Is this the last time that I will see snowflakes as a free man?

As we pull out onto the main highway and head toward the police station, my thoughts return to Olive.

What if she didn't betray me?

What if they were following her and she led them to me by accident?

I unclench my fists and take a breath.

This time my heart doesn't feel like it's splintering into a million different pieces.

Okay, I say to myself. Now what?

I take another breath. Deeper this time. The air flows in and out of my lungs and my body starts to relax even more.

Does this mean...what I want it to mean?

Does this mean that maybe she didn't really betray me?

Maybe they just followed her?

My body certainly seems to think that, and for a moment I let it. But then the rational part of me takes over. This part doesn't care much for feelings and emotions. The only thing that matters is the likelihood of something being true. And in this case?

Yes, perhaps the FBI did have their eye on her. But would they have followed her all the way from California?

Would she *not* have noticed them?

How could they have known that she was coming here? We communicated using burner phones so that our calls were untraceable.

My heart starts to tighten again as the truth comes to the surface. Though it's definitely a possibility that she just led them here, it's unlikely. What's more likely is that Olive knew exactly what she was doing. She had betrayed me, *on purpose*, probably to get back at me for what I did to her.

THE INTERROGATION ROOM is as nondescript and empty of all life as the ones you see on television. There are no windows and only one door.

I expect a two-way mirror but they don't even have that.

Instead, there are two cameras mounted to the ceiling, one facing me (the suspect) and the other facing the interrogator. I'm at the local police station but it is an FBI agent who first comes in.

He is tall and built like a football player, though those days are well behind him. His hair is cut short, straight across the top, a look popular with 1980's TV movie villains. He asks me a series of questions that I have no intention of answering or even justifying with a response. When he sees that he's not getting anywhere, he leaves and sends in a replacement.

Scrawny and lean, he doesn't look much older than thirty and yet I can tell that he has been around the block a few times in his career. He doesn't give off the same goofy vibe as the other one and appears more threatening with his demeanor. If it were anyone else, perhaps I would have felt that way. The first guy was playing the role of a good cop and this one is definitely the bad cop.

"Listen, you don't need to try to scare me," I say, sitting back in the most uncomfortable chair on the planet. "I already told you and the other guy. I want to talk to my lawyer."

"You don't have one," he points out.

"I'm entitled to one, right? This is still America?"

Begrudgingly, the FBI agent nods.

"I would like to call a lawyer and until I have him with me, I'm not saying another word."

The FBI agent whose name I already

forgot folds his arms across his chest and puffs it out in frustration.

"This isn't going to help your case," he finally says. "If you talk to us, and explain, I might be able to help you."

With my arms shackled to each side of the table, I can't move so I just sit up a little and look him straight in the eyes.

"I don't think so, kid," I say slowly and then sit back.

Without another word, he leaves the room.

I look up at the camera and give it a wink. I didn't get far but at least I didn't give them anything that they were looking for.

Cops often don't know as much as they want you to *believe* they do. So, they want to make their case by talking to you. It's tempting, of course. You're in chains and you want to explain how this whole thing is a terrible mistake. But I force myself to keep my mouth shut.

When the doorknob turns, I brace myself for yet another FBI agent.

Good cop didn't work.

Bad cop didn't work.

So, what the hell are they going to throw at me now?

"Hello, Nicholas," Art Hedison says and my heart jumps into my throat.

2

NICHOLAS

WHEN I SEE HIM...

I steel my gaze on him, without looking like I'm scared or even surprised to see him. No, this asshole doesn't deserve a flinch from me.

"How are you doing?" he asks.

My mind rushes through all of the possible explanations and reactions. What should I say? How should I act?

"I'm fine, given the circumstances," I say with a casual shrug. "And you?"

"Good, good," he says, nodding his head.

He stares at me and I stare back.

We both know why he's here. The first two FBI agents couldn't get anything out of me, so he's here to do what they couldn't do.

He is here to make me admit something.

He's here to rattle me.

He's here to break me.

"Are you surprised to see me?"

I shrug.

"I'm sure you are given that you thought that you would never see me again after that day at the mall."

This is what they call 'leading the witness.' I don't take the bait. I just sit back in my chair and lift up my chin in the air.

"You remember that day, Nicholas?"

"I have no idea what you're talking about," I say.

"Are you denying the fact that we met at the mall?" he asks, raising his eyebrows.

My thoughts return to our last meeting. It was out in public with lots of people around and, more importantly, with cameras recording our every move.

"Maybe," I say, tilting my head to one side. "Maybe not. I'm going to tell you what I told the other two agents. I'm not admitting to anything or confirming anything until my lawyer gets here. I know my rights and I intend to use them."

"That would be a very big mistake, Nicholas. 'Cause you see, I can help you. I'm here for you."

Like you were there for me before? I'm tempted to say. What a fucking joke!

"I'm just here to help. I know that you have your side of the story and I know that you didn't kill anyone."

He's tempting me.

He's saying that he believes me when we both know that he doesn't.

And even if he does, it's just a lie anyway. The only reason he's here is to get a confession.

"I know you didn't kill anyone," Art says, leaning closer to me. "The thing is that *they* don't know that."

He nods back at the camera as he says the word 'they.' He's on my side. He's trying to be my friend again.

"I had a choice, Nicholas. They found out about my little indiscretion and Internal Affairs were after me. The only way I could get out of it was to tell them what I know about you."

"This doesn't sound like an apology," I

say, the words escaping my lips before I can stop them.

"I'm sorry. I am," he says, leaning closer to me again. "But I'm here to help you. For real."

I run my fingers over the handcuffs around my wrists and feel the smoothness of the metal.

"I saw you on TV," I say slowly. "You gave interviews to a bunch of different programs always talking about how much of a dangerous criminal I am and that I killed my partner."

The expression on Art's face changes from eager to surprise. He wasn't expecting this.

"What's the matter?" I continue. "Did you think they were broadcasting to some private channel rather than to millions of households around the country? Or did you just not expect me to see it?"

"I had to do that, Nicholas. My boss wanted me to. We had to create buzz around your case. We had to have the public's help in finding you."

I exhale deeply.

"What do you want from me, Art?" I ask.

"I want you to allow me to help you. I know that you didn't kill your partner or your ex-girlfriend."

"Really? 'Cause those charges they read to me say pretty much that exact thing."

Art stares at me. My eyes meet his and neither of us look away.

"They have a strong case, Nicholas. You were with your partner when it happened. You'd just done a big job, it was worth millions. People have killed their partners for a lot less."

He was my best friend I'm tempted to say. I would never do anything like that.

But I force myself to keep my mouth shut.

"You have no alibi for that night. There are eyewitness reports of people who saw you in the area. We even have video recordings of you at a nearby convenience store."

"Is there a reason why you're telling me all of this?" I ask smugly.

"Of course, there is. I want you to understand the case that we have on you. I also want you to know that you can trust me. You need to tell me what really happened so that I can help you get out of this mess."

He's trying to be my friend and, I have to admit, he's doing a good job at it.

"Once your lawyer gets here, I won't be able to help you anymore," he adds.

I laugh.

"What's so funny? You don't believe me?"

"You're just so predicable Art. I thought you'd have a better line than that."

"It's not a line. It's the truth," he insists.

I glare at him again. He waits for me to say something and I wait to gather my thoughts and work out the exact thing that I want to say.

One wrong word can send me to prison for life or worse.

No, when in doubt, keep your fucking mouth shut. That should be the motto of every single person who has ever been arrested.

There is no explaining to the cops.

There is no pandering.

There is no over-extending.

Everything you say can and will be used against you in a court of law, at least in this country. That means it's in your best interest to stay quiet, no matter how much you want to speak up in your defense.

I'm tempted to question their eyewitness reports and their video recordings. I'm tempted to find out more about what they have but they will only share things that will make me even more curious.

"I have no idea what you're talking about," I say, sitting back in my chair. "I'm making another request to see an attorney. I already told the cop in the car on the way over here, the other FBI agents, and you. I'm entitled to representation and that's what I want."

3

OLIVE

WHEN I SEE HIM...

When they pull him away from me and put him into handcuffs, I collapse onto the floor. Two police officers have to hold me up to keep me upright as my legs completely let go. Someone starts talking to me and when I don't respond, another person pipes in. But I don't hear a thing they're saying.

A loud buzzing sound reverberates in my head, blocking all incoming sound. I see their mouths move and I see them tugging at my arms trying to position me here and then there but I don't respond. It's like everything is happening to someone else. Is that possible?

Some time passes before some of the shock wears off. The cops gather in clumps outside, holding their jackets around their necks as the snow starts to fall. I look out of the window to try to get a glimpse of Nicholas but they've taken him to some car out by the road. I can't see him and he can't see me.

What must he be thinking at this moment?

My heart tightens as my breathing becomes more laborious. What if...I don't let myself go there at first. But then I can't stop the thoughts from flooding in.

What if he thinks it's me?

What if he thinks I led them here, *on purpose*?

Someone talks to me again but his words don't get processed. When he hands me my clothes, I put them on. When he hands me my coat, I put that on. When he hands me Solly, I take him in my arms and pet his head, letting out a deep sigh of relief.

In all of the commotion, I actually forgot that I was a mother of a cat. Whatever happens, I need to make sure that he is okay.

A strong gust of wind rushes through my open coat as I step outside. Another cop hands me my hat and I pull the zipper closed to keep some of the cold out.

They show me to a car and put me in the back seat.

I buckle the seat belt and don't bother asking where we're going. They have questions that they want me to answer. Solly purrs under my fingers as I try to figure out what I should and shouldn't tell them about Nicholas.

He's on the FBI's Most Wanted list.

He has a warrant out for his arrest.

The fact that I was found in his trailer, with him, means that they will want to get me for aiding and abetting a fugitive.

Whether or not they can prove this, I am not sure, but what I say to them will be of t paramount importance.

The interrogation room is small and windowless and they allow me to keep Solly in my lap even offering me something to drink. Freezing to my bones, I opt for some hot tea.

The first FBI agent introduces himself

and takes a seat across from me. His eyes look kind as does his demeanor but I know that's all a facade. They are being nice right now because I have something they want.

But what?

Something to help them make a case against Nicholas.

Whatever I say or don't say, I know that I have to protect him. I can't let them frame him for something he didn't do.

"Your boyfriend is in a lot of trouble," the agent says, sitting back in his chair.

"Ex-boyfriend," I correct him even though it hurts me to say the word.

"Is that so? Didn't you spend the night with him?"

"Doesn't mean that we aren't exes," I say, shrugging. "We broke up and that was just a brief reunion, nothing else."

The agent nods but makes it clear that he isn't convinced that I'm telling the truth. My heart starts to race. I rub Solly behind the ears until my blood pressure drops.

"Nicholas Crawford is a dangerous man," the agent says.

"I don't know what you're talking about," I insist.

"He is wanted by the FBI he is, in fact, one of our Ten Most Wanted. I'm sure you've seen the shows—"

"No," I say, shaking my head, looking as much as possible like a deer in headlights.

If I can convince them that I know nothing then that's my best chance of getting out of this mess without any charges.

"There have been programs on 20/20, Dateline, all of the big ones—"

"Like I said," I interrupt him. "I don't watch TV and I had no idea this was going on."

"What is it with your generation and the cord cutting," the agent mutters under his breath. "I mean, what the hell do you do in your spare time if you don't watch TV?"

"I like to read and watch Netflix," I say innocently.

"Tell me what you know about his old partner."

"I don't know much. Nicholas never shared much with me. That's one of the reasons we broke up."

"Oh, really?" someone says, walking into the room. I look past the agent and see that the voice belongs to Art Hedison.

I swallow hard but don't let him see me sweat.

"I happen to know that you and Nicholas are actually very close," Art says, taking a seat in between me and the agent. I shrug.

For a moment, I consider pretending that I don't know who he is but we had met, before his meeting with Nicholas at the mall.

"What's that look on your face, Olive? Don't you remember me?"

"I remember you questioned me about some paintings you thought I stole, which I didn't," I say.

He didn't have any proof and was hoping to get some through his questioning but I didn't give him any. And I won't now.

"Olive, I know that you know that I was working with Nicholas. Everyone knows that."

"No, I don't," I say with a shrug. "I have no idea what you're talking about."

"This is going to go a lot more smoothly if you cooperate. We know that you are not involved with this, so you don't have anything to hide."

"If you know that, then why am I here?" I ask. "What do you want from me?"

"We want you to tell us about Nicholas. Anything you know."

I take a moment to think about that. "I know that he didn't kill anyone," I say. "I know that you have the wrong person."

"We don't think so," Art says, shaking his head, laying out the case that they have against him.

Millions were stolen.

People are killed for a lot less.

There's video surveillance from a nearby store showing him in the area.

I listen to the whole story, thank him, and repeat that I don't know anything about that.

On the outside, I act like I'm made of iron. Nothing can hurt me.

But on the inside, I'm trembling.

What if he did do that horrible thing?

What if Nicholas is a murderer like my brother has thought all along?

Hours pass as we go in circles, getting nowhere.

Two more agents try to get me to open up but I stand my ground. I ask for a lawyer and pressure them to press charges against me or to let me go.

They don't respond and continue to barrage me with questions. Finally, I've had enough.

I get up and say that I'm leaving.

I hold my breath as I walk out of the station, waiting for them to throw a pair of cuffs on me and arrest me but they don't.

4

OLIVE

WHEN I GO BACK HOME...

The cops and the FBI have kept me for hours in their interrogation room, alternating between having me just sit there staring at the walls and telling one person after another that I would like to see an attorney.

Outside, I inhale the cold fresh air of the season's first snowstorm and open my mouth for a snowflake to land on my tongue. When it does, I promise myself that I'm going to find out the truth about Nicholas.

I wrap my coat tighter around Solly to make sure he doesn't catch a chill (can cats get colds? I have no idea) and walk purposely out into the parking lot and then toward the nearest diner.

Twenty-four hours later, I walk down the slushy street outside Logan International Airport looking for my Uber. The driver tries to make small talk but I am too tired to respond. He mentions that I am lucky to get in when I did because they are cancelling flights all along the East Coast, apparently the first big blizzard of the season is about to hit.

I pay his tip on my phone and slug my stuff upstairs. I don't have much besides a small suitcase but it feels like I'm trying to walk two large duffel bags full of bricks all of the way to my apartment.

It doesn't occur to me to knock until I see the surprised look on Sydney's face. I have been gone for a long time. I did start a new life in California and she is definitely not expecting to see me here tonight.

"I'm really sorry," I mumble into her ear. "I didn't mean to interrupt anything, I just had to come home."

After a long embrace, we pull away from each other and she asks how I'm doing.

The question is so loaded, I have no idea how to even begin answering it.

Instead, I take a few steps down the foyer and see that she is playing hostess. Her mother and James are seated around the dining room table with polite expressions on their faces.

I'm tempted to just say a brief hello, introduce them to Solly, and go hide in my room. But I don't want to be rude so I take my cue from Sydney.

I glance at her trying to figure out what she wants me to do. They invite me to join them for dinner and when Sydney gives me the nod of her approval, I agree. It would be a lie to say that I'm not starving. There's freshly ordered Italian food from one of my favorite restaurants and James pours me a big glass of red wine.

The conversation focuses on me and my trip to California with Sydney's mom occasionally interjecting and telling me about her experiences at Palm Springs. Almost two hours later, dinner, dessert, and coffee are finally over and I retire to my room right after everyone leaves.

"What are you doing here?" Sydney bursts in, as I change into loose-fitting pjs and climb under the covers.

"It's a long story."

"Nicholas is custody," she says. "I read about it online."

"So, I guess it's a short one."

"What's going on, Olive?"

I take a deep breath.

"I went to see him. I needed to talk to him. I ended up staying the night..."

"Olive," Sydney admonishes me.

"It's not like that. He's a good person, Syd. It was a mistake."

"He's a con man."

I shake my head.

I mean, it's true but so I am.

And he wasn't conning me. Right?

"They arrested him for murder, Olive. They wouldn't do that if he was innocent."

"They arrest innocent people all the time," I say.

She shifts her weight to her back foot.

She knows that what I'm saying is true, she just doesn't want to admit it.

"How do you know he's innocent?"

I pat the edge of the bed, insinuating for her to sit down.

She does and I tell her everything that has happened that led me to Montana, including how I found Solly. She pets his head and gives him a little kiss while she listens.

"I thought you didn't like cats." I smile.

"Normally, I don't."

"Sydney, I'm here to find out the truth," I say, sitting back against the tufted headboard. "About Nicholas. About what he did and didn't do. I don't think he killed his partner. I don't think he killed his ex-girlfriend but I need to get to the bottom of it. I need to know the truth. I deserve to."

"Of course, you do," she insists. "But how?"

"*That* I have no idea."

We sit silently for a little bit until I pivot the conversation to her.

One of the last times we spoke, she'd caught James cheating on her.

She'd called me in tears, completely distraught, and broken.

But today, he was sitting there with her

mother as if nothing had happened. I played along for her sake when I first came in, not wanting to make a scene, but now I want to know the truth.

"What is going on with James?" I ask.

She looks away from me.

She wants me to change the topic but I refuse.

I simply wait for her to respond. After a few minutes, she takes a deep breath.

"He begged me to take him back," she says quietly.

"And you did?"

"He promised he would never do anything like that again."

"So you forgave him?" I ask.

She shakes her head.

"Why was he here then?"

"My mom," she says quietly.

I stare at her, not fully understanding what she's saying.

"I was about to tell her what happened but she was going on and on about how great he was and how if anything happened, I was going to be the one to screw it up...so I couldn't come out and say it."

My mouth nearly drops open.

"So, are you still together?" I ask.

"He begged me to take him back and I sort of did. For my mom."

"Sydney," I say, shaking my head.

"I didn't want her to be disappointed. I didn't want her to have one more reason to think I was a loser."

"But he's the one who is the loser," I insist. "He's the one who cheated on you. Surely, she would understand that and wouldn't want you to be with someone who cheated on you."

But Sydney just shakes her head. I wrap my arms around her and hold her for a while.

"She would just blame it on me," Sydney finally says when she comes back up for air.

Our eyes meet and I stare into hers trying to understand what the hell she is talking about.

"She would blame me for making him cheat on me," she mumbles. "I didn't want to talk to her about it and I *don't* want to talk about it now."

"Sydney, you have nothing to be ashamed of!" I yell after her as she walks away.

"The wedding is back on," she says, slamming my door behind her.

5

OLIVE

The following morning, we meet again over breakfast. I'm feeling considerably better and pour myself a big bowl of granola. There's no milk so I eat it dry.

Sydney and I make small talk without really addressing what is on our minds. I don't go into the details about what happened with Nicholas and she doesn't discuss James.

I am sure that we are both worried about each other and we both think we're making mistakes, but for now we keep it to ourselves.

"Okay, I can't stand it anymore," I say, finishing my cup of tea and pouring myself some more hot water from the kettle to fill it back up. "I know that you think that Nicholas did something wrong, but he didn't. At least, I don't think so and I'm back here to find out the truth."

"What are you going to do?"

"I have no idea, but I'm going to try to find his friends from back home and just get to the bottom of this somehow."

"That's a bad idea," Sydney says unceremoniously as if I don't know that already.

The people he associated with back then were mafia members, at best, and cold-blooded murderers at worst. Who the hell knows what kind of dealings they were involved in and who the hell knows what they'll do to me to get to him? I know this, probably more than Sydney does.

But I have to try.

I don't have any other choice.

Otherwise, I won't be able to forgive myself.

"You're an idiot if you do this," Sydney says, grabbing a handful of granola out of the box and stuffing it into her mouth.

"Of course, I am," I say with a shrug. "I'm a woman in love."

"Oh, don't be like that." She shakes her head. "Don't be stupid."

"I have to find out the truth about Nicholas. I love him and I can't just continue loving him and not know. If he did it then it's over, but if he didn't then I will fight for him."

Sydney gets up and goes to the sink. She turns her body away from mine and I sense that something is wrong by the way her shoulders tense up.

"What? What is it?" I ask. She doesn't reply so I try again.

"He's going to go away for a very long time, Olive. Years. I just don't want you to be one of those women who visits their loved ones in prison. It's awful. I know that TV makes it look romantic but it's shit. You know it. I know it."

I've never thought about that until she brought it up.

Shivers run down my spine.

What if that happens?

What if I find out the truth and he's innocent and that's still not enough?

What if they have a trial and convict him anyway?

My blood runs cold.

I crack my knuckles and stare at the floor.

SYDNEY and I don't talk much after that. I escape to my room until she goes to work and try to figure out what to do. I have no idea who Nicholas hung out with back then and even if I could reach him, there is no way he would ever name names.

He would just tell me to stay away, which is probably wise advice, except that you can never find out a thing by not asking difficult questions.

There is, however, one person who might know.

I look her up on Facebook and when I message her, she responds pretty quickly.

She messages her address and, an hour later, I find myself walking down a street in a very nice part of town near Cambridge where the luxury condos tower over the sidewalks and slim moms, with fifteen-hundred dollar strollers, exercise in the park.

I look up the address a few more times, double-checking that I am going to the right place. This is the last place I expected her to live.

Nicholas only told me a few things about his mom and how he was raised, but the one thing I know for sure is that he didn't grow up with money. And this building has new money written all over it.

A doorman opens the door for me and asks who I am here to see. I tell him her name and after a polite smile he makes a call to her apartment. A few minutes later, I stand in front of her door.

I knock twice and hold my breath.

"Coming!" she yells from somewhere deep in the apartment. It takes her a few minutes to get here.

"Olive?" she asks abruptly as she opens the door.

"Yes, thank you for seeing me, Mrs. Crawford."

Nicholas' mom waves her hand and invites me inside. There's a cigarette in between her two fingers and, with her other hand, she drags an oxygen tank on two wheels behind her. It makes a loud sound on the hardwood floor and I wonder if it will cause damage after continuous use.

The apartment itself is gorgeous.

There are floor-to-ceiling windows looking out onto the park below. The furniture looks like it's straight out of the West Elm catalog. The only thing that doesn't seem to fit is Mrs. Crawford.

She's not very old but very overweight. There are fast food wrappers everywhere along with empty liquor bottles and beer cans. On the console table behind the couch, I spot pill bottles. She may not be actively trying to kill herself but I'm not sure she's not going to succeed at it at this rate.

"What do you want?" Mrs. Crawford asks me.

"Um..." I stutter, not sure where to start.

"You said you were Nicky's girlfriend and you had some news for me."

"Oh, yes, of course." I nod.

I look around her place and again forget what I came here for.

This apartment must cost four grand a month, at least.

Where does she get this kind of money?

Has Nicholas been supporting her?

"If you're not going to talk, you best get out of my house," Mrs. Crawford barks at me.

.

6

OLIVE

WHEN I TALK TO HER...

Get yourself together, I say to myself. You came here to find something out so don't act like a deer in headlights and make her think you're an idiot. If you want to find out who Nicholas was friends with, you have to give her something first.

"Sorry, I'm just a little distressed over everything that has happened," I say, clearing my throat.

"What do you mean?" Mrs. Crawford asks, dragging on her cigarette.

"Well, you see, Nicholas got arrested."

"Arrested?" She smirks.

I thought she would be surprised but instead she just sits down on the couch and shakes her head and laughs. Her laugh is thick and throaty, forming somewhere in the deep of her stomach and coming out like a crackle. Instead of joy, it's full of contempt.

"They arrested him for supposedly killing his old partner from the streets but I don't think he did it," I say, trying another approach.

Surely, she doesn't think her son is capable of anything like this.

She takes another drag on her cigarette and adjusts her over-sized nightgown that zips up the front. It has large pink flowers on it adding to its general shapelessness, though it's probably quite comfortable.

"Eh, who the hell knows what that kid is capable of," she says.

"He didn't do this, Mrs. Crawford," I insist.

"You don't know that. You don't know the first thing about my son."

I refuse to accept that, even though a small part of me sort of believes her. Still, I can't let her know this.

"He promised to pay for this apartment. He put me in here. Said that my old neighborhood is shit and I should live somewhere else. I agree. But now what? He hasn't sent me rent in two months. One more and they're going to start eviction proceedings, if they haven't yet. And then I'm going to have to move again. Do you know what that's like for a woman my age?"

"I'm really sorry about that, Mrs. Crawford."

I am not sure what else to say. I was about to ask her about his old friends when she went on this rant and now it only feels right to acknowledge her predicament.

"Do you have any money?" she asks.

Her bluntness makes me take a step back as if her words were actually a physical blow.

"No...um, no, I don't."

She looks me up and down, analyzing the value of my shoes up to my coat and scarf.

"I'm not so sure about that."

I have no idea what exactly she saw in my attire but it definitely doesn't reflect like I have more than twenty bucks to spend on the whole ensemble.

"Let me assure you, I don't have any

money. And frankly, I didn't even realize that Nicholas had any."

This last part is a lie and I immediately regret saying it as soon as the words escape my mouth. She narrows her eyes and tilts her head to one side. She isn't buying it.

"My son always has money, even if he says he doesn't," she hisses. "Or at the very least, he has a way to get some."

I take a deep breath. My current approach of taking my time and trying to lead her into the conversation that I want to have isn't working well. It's time for me to pivot.

"Mrs. Crawford, Nicholas has been arrested for murder. I doubt that he's going to get out on bail."

"What do you want from me?" she asks when I pause for a moment trying to gather my thoughts.

"I need you to tell me where I can find some of his old friends from back then. The people he used to hang out with. Someone must know what happened. The truth of what happened."

"Yeah, he killed his partner to keep the

whole loot," she says with a smirk. "What the fuck do you think happened?"

"I need to find out the truth."

"That is the truth," she spits back. "You're wasting your time."

"Even if I am, can you please just tell me where I can find them? Anyone."

She takes a long drag of her cigarette and walks over to the window. The oxygen tank makes a loud squeaking sound as it rolls over the parquet floors.

"Come here," she says, indicating for me to approach her with her index finger. I do as she says.

"You see that BMW down there, all covered in snow?" I look at where she's pointing and see a new model BMW SUV parked at the corner.

"Nicholas got me that car when he got me this apartment," she says.

Unsure as to how to respond, I mumble that he's a good son.

"Good son? You think so?" she snaps.

When my eyes meet hers, all I see is anger and hatred.

"It's a lease, you idiot. This apartment is a

rental. If he really loved me, he would've bought these things outright. But he didn't, because he's a selfish prick who doesn't think of anyone but himself."

I feel like the wind has been knocked out of me.

I want to defend him but I don't want to make her angry. I need her to tell me what she knows. So, I bite my tongue and just listen.

"I really need to find his old friends, Mrs. Crawford," I say. "Maybe they'll have some answers for me so I can help him get out of prison."

"You really don't know who you are messing with, girlie," she says. "Those guys don't talk. They're in the mob. They don't turn on each other."

"That's not what I want them to do. I just want them to give me some information that might help him."

She shakes her head and lights another cigarette.

"You're wasting your time."

"Maybe I am, but I have to do something," I say. Sensing that I'm not getting through, I search for another approach.

"And if by some chance I can get him out, I'm sure that he'll be happy to pay your rent and car payments again."

I can tell that I have hit on something by the way her eyes light up as if there's a bulb flashing over her head. Finally, she has a reason to help.

"There's a clubhouse they used to all meet at. It's in South Boston, nowhere a pretty girl like you should ever step foot in. I have no idea if they still meet there but they are creatures of habit," Mrs. Crawford says, putting out her cigarette. "But I've got to warn you, if you go there, you'll be a sheep walking into a wolf's den. And I don't say that lightly."

7

OLIVE

WHEN I MAKE A DECISION...

I don't think much of Nicholas' mother and I can see why he never introduced me to her before. I knew that his relationship with her was as complicated as my relationship with my own mother and sometimes the best thing to do in situations like ours is to just bury our grief and disappointment deep inside. I know that's not the healthy thing to do, but it's often the easiest.

The one thing that I have been debating whether or not to bring up was Ashley. I needed her to tell me the truth about his old friends and I may need to follow up with her again, so I can't bring myself to say everything I thought about her for what she did to my best friend.

Ashley had gone through so much and she kept all of her sorrows bottled up within her.

I wish that she could've opened up to me just once, perhaps then there would've been something I could've done.

This was my opportunity to say something to the woman who hurt her but I didn't do it. Not because I didn't want to, but because I didn't want to burn a bridge I might need to use in the future.

Later that evening, curled up on my bed, I consider my options.

I have looked up the cross streets of the clubhouse that she told me about online and examined the exterior on Google Maps. I walked virtually up and down the street trying to find out as much as I could about what I am about to walk into. There is no real-time video recording data, of course, so it's hard to know what kind of men I can expect to meet there.

Nicholas' mom warned me that they will not be happy to see me and that will make it even worse. Nicholas double-crossed them a long time ago and they will view me as a way to get even with him. There's only one problem with that plan. Nicholas is locked up and he's not getting out unless they give me some information.

I'm tempted to tell Sydney where I'm going and to ask for her help but I'm afraid she will do everything in her power to stop me.

Still, I can't just walk in there without some sort of way to protect myself.

No, I need a gun.

I need to buy one and then teach myself how to use it.

But if I want to use it and have it not be traced back to me, I can't have it registered in my name.

I search for "how to buy a gun online" and read about all of the regulations, or lack thereof, that exist.

A few pages into the search results, I stumble upon forums where people can sell each other weapons without going through licensed dealers.

As I go deeper and deeper down the

wormhole, I quickly find posts by owners selling guns without identification numbers and those willing to ship them to anyone, even those who state that they can't pass any background checks.

After messaging with a few different people using my burner phone and a fake name, I find one who is willing to meet up with me to do the exchange.

I consider having them mail it to me but I'd like to go there tomorrow. Needing a safe place to meet, I suggest Starbucks.

Later that evening, after waiting for my chai latte, a middle-aged man with the collar of his pea coat pulled up starts to make small talk with me.

I had been eyeing the rotund man in the corner hiding behind his laptop thinking that he might be the seller, but it turns out that it's this sophisticated-looking man with polished black shoes.

Neither of us ask any questions. Instead, he opens the bag that he has slung across his body and unfolds the brown wrapping paper around it.

I peek over his shoulder, assessing the

merchandise. Ideally, I could take it out and feel it in my hand but in this case, I have to take the word of a complete stranger.

I dig into my own purse and pull out an envelope with the four hundred in cash. He counts it quickly by placing it in his bag and opening the envelope out of sight of wandering eyeballs.

Once I place the gun, still wrapped firmly in paper, into my satchel, the exchange is complete. He gives me a brief nod and walks out of the door, dumping his drink in the garbage can on the corner.

Meanwhile, I melt into the chair at the far end of the corner. I put the bag firmly against my thigh, taking a sip of my drink and spilling part of it on myself. Watching my hands clean up the mess, I finally see exactly how much they are still shaking.

But it's not just the gun that's scaring me, it's the fact that I might have to use it. And sometime soon.

8

OLIVE

WHEN I GO THERE...

Initially, I thought I would make my way to the clubhouse the day after I bought the gun, but that evening, I decide that I need more time to prepare.

I haven't held a gun in my hands since I was a little girl and my uncle showed me how to shoot his rifle. I spend the evening practicing loading and unloading the clip and putting in the bullets I had bought at Walmart, following along with the instructions on YouTube.

One of the videos mentions that if I don't want the gun traced then I can file off the number and exactly how to do it using things I have in my garage (as if I have a garage). But checking my gun, I see that I got a good deal: the last owner had already done this, just like he said he would.

The following morning I take a bus to a gun range across town. From the online reviews I know that they don't ask for identification and it's a good place if you want to keep to yourself as you shoot.

The practice goes as well as can be expected. I'm not a good shot but I review the right technique from the YouTube videos I saved and make sure to follow their instructions explicitly. By the end of my hour there, I'm at least hitting the target even if it's not right in the center.

The following day I put on a thick black jacket (vegan leather!), which I found at one of my favorite thrift stores and take two buses to the clubhouse that Nicholas' mom told me about. I'm tempted to use an Uber but buses are harder to track just in case something happens.

Dressed in jeans and ankle boots, I glance at myself in the window of an empty storefront.

What the hell am I doing? I say silently to myself.

What is my plan exactly?

To just go in there, tell them who I am, and demand that they tell me what they know about Nicholas' life back then?

Why would they do that?

Besides, even if one of them is willing to speak to me, would he in front of his friends?

It feels like a terrible idea, but I don't have a better one. I don't know what is on the other side of that door and I can't just wait out on the curb to ask people questions who come out. There's probably more than one way in and out and I don't want one of them warning the others that I'm coming.

I crack my knuckles trying to get some blood circulating in my frozen hands. It's not particularly cold out here, but my anxiety is making my whole body shiver.

"Okay, no more waiting, it's now or never," I mumble under my breath.

The door to the clubhouse is so worn that the wood is soft to the touch, full of nicks and indentations from years of use. I turn the aging brass knob quickly out of fear that if I don't then I won't at all.

On the inside, the place looks like a bar. Dimly lit. No windows to speak of. A large bar top dominates the space and bottles of liquor are behind it.

I had assumed that the people would all be here, right behind the door, but there isn't a soul around. I'm tempted to yell out, "Hello?" But then I stop myself. If I want to get answers, I need the element of surprise.

Unsure as to what to do now, I walk down the creaky floorboards toward the opening down the hallway. For all I know, Nicholas' mom might have been lying to me the whole time.

Why not, right? And if she did, then where the hell am I?

"Who are you?" his deep voice comes directly behind me. I snap my head back but he already has my arms locked behind me.

"Who are you?" he hisses into my ear.

"I'm...Olive Kernes....I'm looking for Ricky."

"Ricky who?" he asks, fighting his grip around my arms.

"Ricky Trundell."

He loosens his grip and pushes me down the hallway.

"Hey, what are you doing?" I resist and try to push back at him.

He's too strong to resist full-on, so instead I let my legs drop and my body go limp. Now, he'll have to physically carry me if he wants me to go somewhere.

"What the hell?" the man asks, when his grip slips and I fall onto the floor. I scramble to my feet and pull the gun out of my pocket.

"Get the fuck away from me," I say, holding it as steady as I can. Luckily, he takes me seriously and takes a step away from me.

"Where can I find Ricky Trundell?" I ask.

The hallway is dark and all I can see is the white of his eyes.

"I don't think you know what you're doing, little girl," the man mocks me.

"Tell me where Ricky is," I say without missing a beat.

I'm at a point where all I can do is pretend that I know what I'm doing. A facade is better than nothing. They don't know anything about me and they just might believe it.

"Back there," the man finally caves. I let out a slight, but hopefully unnoticeable, sigh of relief.

"Come with me," I say. I take a few steps back, keeping the gun squarely on him. He follows my instructions.

The door leading to the back room is slightly ajar and I push it open with my back. As soon as I turn to face the table, all four men rise to their feet and point their weapons in my face.

"Told ya this was a bad idea." The man who grabbed me starts to laugh.

"I'm here just to ask you some questions," I say, trying to defuse the situation.

"Who the hell do you think you are?" the tall one with a scar across his face asks.

"I need your help," I say sternly.

I drop the gun to my side but don't let go of it.

The men continue to point their guns in my face until the older man in a worn leather jacket and a cigar in between his fingers raises his palm and waves it a little, telling them to lower them. One of them tries to protest his decision, but he just gives them one hard look and the man caves.

"Who are you?" he asks.

"My name is Olive Kernes and I'm looking for Ricky Trundell."

"Why?"

"I need to ask him a few questions."

"Are you a fucking cop?" one of the young guys to my left yells out. "Have you completely lost your mind?"

"I'm not a cop. I don't work with law enforcement. I'm here about something else."

"What?"

They all stare at me as I try to decide whether or not I should just come out and say it. One of them takes a sip of his beer and another taps his fingers slightly on the table.

They are all dressed in dark clothes; leather jackets and black pants. It's not a uniform per se, but I wonder if it's a coordinated effort.

"You better speak up," the man in charge says. "I'm not going to wait forever."

9

OLIVE

WHEN I TELL THEM THE TRUTH...

I swallow hard and then tell them that I'm Nicholas Crawford's girlfriend. I tell them that he has been arrested for the murder of his partner and I'm here trying to find out the truth of what happened.

"Nicholas Crawford! Wow, now that's a blast from the past," he says, sitting back in his chair. "We haven't heard that name in these parts in a long time."

Not knowing the best way to respond, I give him a slight nod.

"So, the FBI arrested him, huh?"

"Yes, and that's why I'm here."

"No, you're not." He laughs, running his fingers through his thinning hair.

"What do you mean?"

"Well, you said you were here to find out the truth but that's not true. You're here to find evidence, if you can call it that, that exonerates him."

"Yes," I admit. "I guess so."

"You know, of course, that Nicholas didn't exactly do right by us, right?"

Frankly, I don't even know their names let alone what Nicholas did or didn't do.

"I don't know the details," I admit. "And I don't really want to know."

I add the last bit because the truth is that I don't want to know. The less I know about these men the better. I don't even want to know their names. All I want to know is what Ricky knows about what happened.

"Smart girl," the boss says, raising his eyebrows. "So, what makes you think that Ricky knows anything about this? Or that Ricky is even here?"

"It's a hunch," I lie.

"Just a hunch?" He starts to laugh, tilting his whole head back and letting the waves of laughter rush through his body all at once.

"I don't care about anything that you have

going on. I just know that Nicholas didn't kill his partner and I need to find any information I can to help him."

"Well, you don't really know if he killed him or not," the boss points out.

He has said that before and hearing it again makes my blood run cold. But I keep my feelings to myself.

"Will you help me?" I ask, getting tired of the games.

The boss narrows his eyes.

"Ricky, are you here?" I ask the room.

I scan their dead, expressionless faces but no one even looks up at me.

"I need to speak to you. I know you know something," I insist.

This is a lie, of course. I know very little about anything that has happened before. The only reason I even know Ricky's name is that it's the only one that Nicholas' mom dropped.

He was a good friend of Nicholas back then and if anyone were to know anything it would be him, she said.

The boss gets up, takes one drag of his cigar before putting it gently on the ashtray.

Then he walks over to me and positions himself as close to me as possible without actually touching. My whole body recoils into itself as I try to get away from him without actually making a move.

"I think it's best that you leave now," he says after a moment.

Now, as if they had been given permission, the guys let themselves loose on me.

"Yeah, get out of here!" one yells.

"Who the hell does she think she is coming here and asking us to help that asshole?"

"Hope he rots in prison!"

"If he ever gets out, he better watch his back!"

I don't make a move to leave.

"Ricky! Are you here? Ricky!" I plead.

I watch their faces and see one of them shy away from me. He looks a little bit like a kid who doesn't want his name called in class because he doesn't know the answer.

Could that be Ricky?

"Olive, you need to leave," the boss says, leaning his head toward mine. He has a svelte and distinguished face but his eyes are bloodshot and menacing.

I decide not to push my luck. The men are all armed and this isn't exactly a friendly situation. If any of them want to talk to me, they are not going to do it while they are in the middle of this group.

When I turn to walk away, someone yells, "And don't come back!" after me.

I TAKE the bus back to my apartment and get my car. Then I drive right back over. I don't really have the intention of coming back here and trying to push for more answers from hostile men, but I don't know what else to do.

The *supposed* murder happened years ago and there were no witnesses. The only thing I have to go on was that at the time, Nicholas was friends with that guy named Ricky and he may have some insight as to what *might* have happened.

The same reasoning that brought me here keeps me here.

I sit in my car, parked on the street

opposite the clubhouse. There isn't much street parking here but if the rest of the block wasn't abandoned with empty storefronts then there might have been some competition for spaces.

Rain starts to fall.

Big thick drops collide with my windshield and the ill-functioning windshield wipers do little to make the visibility better.

After a few moments, I give up entirely and shut the engine off.

I sit in the car for a long time trying to figure out what to do.

What if I do find out the truth and the truth points to Nicholas being guilty?

What do I do then?

Does that mean that it's over?

Do I just let him go? Perhaps.

The thing is that right now I believe, or maybe just want to believe, that he's innocent. But if I had proof to the contrary? Would I still feel the same way about him? Would anyone?

I take a deep breath and bury my face in my phone.

I need a distraction.

I need something else to think about but my mind seems to be hijacked. Instead of complying and laughing at funny cat and dog videos on YouTube, my thoughts keep going back to Nicholas. When I manage to push some of him out, I come back to Owen.

Owen is another man who has disappointed me, in a long succession of disappointing men.

Maybe I should have known better but, how could I?

I trusted him and he played such a good game.

When he was in prison, he appeared to be rehabilitated. He learned to read and write and wrote me the most eloquent letters. None of them mentioned love or obsession or any of those thoughts that I now know that he had.

I thought that he was my brother and I knew that he needed help.

How could I have known he would turn on me so quickly?

How could I have known that he would be one of my biggest regrets?

Hours pass slowly when you're sitting in the small seat of an old car. First, I listen to music until I get bored and then switch around different audiobooks. I wish I could read but then I could miss them coming and going so I try to put the phone away and not even browse social media.

And then, suddenly, after about the fifth time that I give up hope and plan to drive away, I see *him*.

Same leather jacket.

Same blank look on his face, but with just a tinge of the eagerness some guys have in their teens.

He walks out of the front door and heads north down the street.

My car is facing the same direction so I just wait for him to get a little bit ahead of me before pulling out.

At the corner, he turns left and a few moments later, I do as well.

And then I lose him.

Where did he go? I search the street up and down.

There isn't a soul around and he couldn't have just vanished into thin air!

Did he go into another building?

Shit, shit, shit, I mutter to myself silently.

There are only a few cars on the street and I look them over again. This time, however, I see what I couldn't have known.

Ricky must have leaned over and got something out of his glove box when I see him move in between the two seats.

When he starts his old El Camino, I'm careful to scrunch down behind the wheel and even put on a pair of sunglasses to keep him from recognizing me.

I follow Ricky out of the neighborhood and then out of the city. He drives a good forty-five minutes, all the way to the newer suburbs and then pulls up to a brick apartment building.

It has a number of apartments, with the doors all facing the streets. Little kids play on the playground in front of the parking lot.

I find a spot at the very end and watch him walk up the exposed staircase to the top floor and knock on the door of the apartment number 23.

A moment later, the door opens and he walks inside.

I sink back into my seat.

What the hell do I do now?

I had assumed that Ricky was going home and that I would be able to talk to him one-on-one, but now looking at this place and how far away it is from everywhere, I'm not so sure.

What if I had followed him to a job?

What if he's doing something he's not supposed to against the organization?

Or, what if he's doing something illegal that he was instructed to do and now here I am witnessing those illegal dealings?

My heart races and my head pounds and I grip the steering wheel harder and harder until my hands feel like they're going to break.

10

OLIVE

WHEN I ASK FOR HIS HELP...

I wait a little bit outside of that apartment. At first, I wait for him to come out soon. If he emerges then he might just be there on a job and that's not anything I want to get involved with. I don't know exactly what kind of business Ricky is in, but I know enough to know that it's better for me to be as ignorant of all of those dealings as possible.

When an hour turns into two, I am pretty certain that he is no longer conducting business. He either lives here or is visiting someone who lives here.

I glance at the time. It's almost nine-thirty at night.

If I wait much longer then it will be

almost too late for me to knock on the door and have it still be a decent hour. I don't want to risk having them go to bed and waking them up or interrupting them in any way.

No, it's now or never.

Or rather, it's now or tomorrow morning.

The problem, however, is that I have no idea when Ricky starts work and I have no interest in spending the night in this tin box.

My hand shakes when I make a fist to knock on the door. At first, I hit it so slightly that it barely makes a sound. I take a breath and do it again.

This time they hear me. Or rather, the dog does.

The yelps are loud and thunderous but the voice isn't very deep so I suspect it belongs to someone small.

After a few barks, the loud sound of a baby crying pierces through my ear drum and I immediately regret my decision.

I have made a mistake.

When the woman answers the door, my suspicions are confirmed. My knock woke up the dog who woke up the baby. The woman looks tired and out of sorts and mumbles something about them not being interested in buying anything.

"I'm so sorry, ma'am," I say. "But I'm not selling anything."

"We're not interested in being converted either," she snaps and tries to close the door.

She's in a somewhat precarious position, trying to both calm the screaming baby and keep the dog from escaping using just her foot, so I don't want to press on the door and force it open.

"I'm actually here to talk to Ricky. Is he home?"

Her expression changes immediately.

She no longer looks annoyed but pissed off.

Her eyes get small and laser-like and she gives her dog a stern kick to push her away from the door. Even the baby seems to stop crying for a moment.

"Are you kidding me?" the woman snaps. "Are you seriously coming here *to my house* in the middle of the night?"

"Um..." I mumble, not sure what she is referring to.

"What the hell do you want?" she asks,

pushing her stringy unwashed hair out of her face.

Dressed in sweats and with bags under her eyes, she looks the epitome of a new mother.

"I'm not sure who you think I am—" I start to say but she cuts me off.

"I know who you are. You're the slut he knocked up. Is that why you're here? You want money?"

Dumbfounded, I shake my head.

"No, no," I say. "You have me confused with someone else. I'm not his...anything. I just have a few questions to —"

"Shut up! I don't want to hear it!" she yells and throws something at me.

It hits me straight on the forehead, but it's light and small and does little but stun me.

When the door closes, I figure that that's it. She won't let me see Ricky and I can't really get past her to get to him. But then it opens up again.

The light from the living room wraps around his face, obscuring most of it. All I can make out is a little bit of the mustache and the thick dark curls.

"Why did you follow me here?" Ricky asks.

"I need to talk to you, please."

He raises one eyebrow as if he's considering it but then shuts me down. His wife says something in the background while the baby cries and the dog barks.

"Please, it won't take long," I try again.

"You need to leave." Ricky shuts the door in my face.

I walk back down the stairs in a state of shock. Normally, I'd cry either from anger or frustration or both but on this occasion for some reason I can't.

I just feel lost and confused.

I kick myself for going up there and creating this hostile situation. Maybe if I hadn't then he would be more likely to speak to me. On the other hand, he wasn't particularly willing to before, so perhaps that didn't make things any worse.

When I get back in the car, I start the engine and put the car in reverse. But I can't make myself go.

I can't make myself do it.

I look back to make sure that there's no

one coming behind and check the mirror as well but I can't force myself to step on the accelerator.

Something is keeping me here.

Did I try hard enough?

Did I give up too easily?

11

OLIVE

WHEN WE TALK...

This time hours fly by.

I find a few granola bars in the bottom of my purse and quench some of my hunger. Luckily, I always carry water with me and there are two bottles in the back.

The first hour, I spend perusing through Facebook and Instagram, looking at beautiful pictures of sunsets and tan lines and white beaches. It wasn't that long ago that this life was a very real possibility to me. But what now?

I recline the seat and turn up one of Charlotte Byrd's audiobooks. The book is anything but boring, but the narrator's smooth voice puts me at ease and I can't help but let myself drift away.

A loud thump on my window shakes me out of a deep sleep and it takes me a few moments to remember where the hell I am.

He knocks again.

When my vision comes into focus a little more, I see his mustache and the beginnings of a beard and realize that it is Ricky.

"You shouldn't be here," he says when I roll down the window just a little bit. "This isn't a good neighborhood."

He walks around the car and I unlock the passenger door. A burst of cold air rushes into the car until he closes it.

"Thank you for coming to see me," I say, turning my body toward his.

"You're quite persistent."

It's less of an observation and more of an accusation.

"I'm sorry about how I went about all of this, but I really needed to speak to you. Mrs. Crawford told me that you were very close friends with Nicholas and you might know something."

He bites on the inside of his cheek and

looks out of the window. At least, he's listening, I say to myself and take a deep breath.

"Nicholas has been arrested for the death of his partner, David Kendrick. The FBI thinks they have a case against him, but it's all based on the words of a crooked agent who probably committed much worse crimes."

Ricky shakes his head as he taps his hand on his knee.

"What? Is it not true?" I ask.

"You don't know who Nicholas was back then," he says after a moment.

"And you don't know who he is now," I insist.

"People don't change," Ricky says, waving his hand in my direction.

I feel frustration building up within me but I don't let it boil over. I'm here to ask him questions about what he knows and to find out the truth, not to convince him about the man that Nicholas is now.

"Nicky and I came into the organization about the same time. He rose through the ranks quickly because the bosses liked him."

"Was that his boss, earlier today?" I ask.

"No, different guy. At that time, we didn't really know who was in charge because that was just the way the organization was set up. The less people knew about what we were doing, the better."

I give him a slight nod, encouraging him to keep going.

"Nicky and David were put in charge of insurance scams. They were quite good at that and made a bit of profit doing it."

I have always wondered how much of what Owen told me about Nicholas was true and now at least part of it is confirmed.

"Nicky vanished a day after David showed up dead," Ricky says. "At first, no one thought anything about it. Thought that maybe they just went down to Florida to blow off some steam, celebrate. Not everyone was in the position to do that kind of thing, but the bosses liked them. Well, that didn't turn out to be the case. We quickly found out that David was dead and Nicky was gone."

Owen's story reverberates in my mind as it is almost identical to what Ricky just told me.

"Afterward, we found out that they had a side job going, breaking into wealthy homes, usually ones that are closed up for the season," Ricky continues.

"Do you know what happened to David?" I ask quietly, bracing myself for what he is about to say to me.

Ricky tilts his head from one side to another, as if he is cracking his neck.

"No, I don't," he finally says.

"Do you think Nicholas did it?"

"Nicky was good at his job but he had one major flaw for a mob guy. He wasn't very good at hurting people."

I glance up at him.

"Yeah, you can only go so far in this business if you refuse to take a few lives. That's why the insurance scams worked out so well for him. He always started the fires when no one was around and he was so careful, no one ever got hurt."

"But maybe David did something to make him angry? Turn on him? People get killed for a variety of reasons."

Ricky laughs.

"You seem to have more of an

understanding of what kind of moral flexibility this business requires than Nicky ever did."

I shake my head. "So, what are you saying exactly?" I ask.

"Nicky never hurt anyone. And he certainly would never hurt David, his best friend. He even took a bullet for him."

My mouth nearly drops open.

"Nicky is as loyal as people get. There's no way he would ever do anything like that let alone for something as stupid as a bit of money."

I sit back in my seat taking in everything that he has just said. Suddenly, the pieces of the puzzle all come together in one moment. I realize that I had known the real Nicholas Crawford all along. I thought I needed facts in order to prove what my intuition told me but now it's nothing but a confirmation.

"But how do you know for sure?" I ask, still searching for something that resembles proof.

Ricky waits for a moment. "He was with me the night that it happened," he says slowly.

I furrow my brows and wait for him to continue.

"I knocked off a liquor store and the cops were after me. Nicky hid me. I didn't know they did that job until later."

I lick my lips and pick at the fabric around the steering wheel.

"But how could you know he didn't kill him before you called or after?" I ask. I believe him but my rational mind is looking for details that the prosecution definitely will.

"David's body was found at six a.m. in the marsh by a dog walker. Nicky was with me from six the previous night."

I nod, still looking for loopholes. I try to remember what I read about decomposition science and how inaccurate and imprecise it can be given the cold and other conditions. When I bring this up, Ricky just shakes his head.

"None of that matters," Ricky says. "I was with him and I was there when he heard the news of David's death. I saw him break down and that's when I knew for sure that he had nothing to do with it."

I swallow hard.

"I've never seen him that distraught," Ricky continues. "He kept sobbing and just asking why over and over again."

Ricky looks away from me and out at the bright yellow moon hovering in the distance.

"He just kept saying, 'It was just money. Why would anyone kill him over money?' What Nicky never got was that money is the main reason why people kill anyone."

We sit in silence for a while, not so much enjoying each other's company but rather just tolerating it. I turn up the heat but it doesn't really warm me up no matter how much the hot air blasts in my face. Ricky reaches over and closes the vents on his side of the car.

"What do I do now?" I ask. "Why is the FBI blaming Nicholas?"

Ricky shrugs.

"Is it because of Art? But he helped him out of a pretty big jam."

"You just answered your own question," Ricky says. "He has been crooked for years and there's an Internal Affairs case open on him. They got him for something and he needed to give them something bigger in return. So, he came up with this."

I consider that for a moment, but it doesn't add up.

"Not to be rude, but David was just a smalltime mob guy, why would they care about that? Or at least, why would they consider it a big case at all?"

Ricky shakes his head.

"But it's not just that case that they arrested him for, huh? What about the girl? They probably think they've got themselves a serial killer and there's nothing more sexy to law enforcement officers than serial killers."

"So what do you think I should do now?" I ask. He shrugs his shoulders and gets out of the car.

"Good luck," he says. "Remember, we never had this conversation."

12

NICHOLAS

WHEN I ASK FOR HIS HELP...

The water feels good running down my naked body. It's warm and comforting and, for a few moments, it allows me to forget that I don't have my freedom.

Everyone here watches everything and I'm not just talking about the guards. We all watch each other; every move and every word.

I've made a few friends but it's hard to know if they are my actual friends or if they will turn on me at some convenient point in the future in order to get something.

Very few people in here admit they are guilty of the crimes they committed, but most of them have. I'm still technically in jail, not prison, so there are those who are serving the sentence and those still awaiting trial or plea deals.

When anyone asks, I tell them that I didn't kill those people they accused me of, but no one believes me, not even those I would consider friends.

I open my eyes and watch the water run down from the shower head onto my skin.

Today, I'm alone in here and for a moment I'm suddenly reminded of being home again.

I try to remember what it was like to hold Olive in my arms and transport myself to the last time that we were together; the night before, not during the arrest.

I miss her.

There's no other way around it.

No matter how much I try to convince myself that I should forget her, I can't.

I know that it was she who turned me in and yet I still somehow forgive her.

I love her and that's what love is, right? Or maybe I'm being an idiot.

I DON'T HEAR them coming until they are already here. Through the water rushing past my eyes, I see them. There's four of them and they're dressed.

Somewhere in the corner, I see the guard.

He's lurking, waiting for it to happen. He knew about this before I did and he has no intention of stopping them. I don't know if it's because he doesn't like me or if he just likes them better.

The first blow lands on my stomach. I fold in half from the pain and my feet slip.

I catch myself on the wall and stop myself from falling down.

The second fist collides with my head. It throws me off my feet as I hit the tile behind me.

The ones that follow, I can't remember very well. Everything becomes a blur.

I try to block the blows as best as I can by putting up my forearms into the air in front of my face, but they quickly get heavy and tired yet the blows keep coming.

The men take turns attacking me while they call me filthy things. I can hear the hatred and the anger in their voices and I can't help but wonder what I've ever done to them. And after that, things get even more bleak.

When men are cooped up together in a dark place like this, their sexual urges become a game of power play. And some of them will do anything to satisfy their desires.

The assault goes on for a long time, how long I don't know.

Instead, I just wait for it to end.

A while later, when I think it can't possibly go on any longer, they surprise me and it does. I keep fighting, but it's all to no avail. They use their fists and legs and other parts of their bodies until I'm exhausted and completely spent and then one of them punches me so hard I black out completely.

SOMETIME LATER, I regain consciousness in the infirmary. My eyelids feel too heavy to lift so I keep them closed. There are people rushing around me and other prisoners somewhere on other cots, also shackled to their beds.

One of the nurses is talking to another just within earshot. At first, I can't make out their words but slowly I start to put pieces of their conversation together.

"You know that you have something to live for, right?" one of them says, talking to the guy next to me about him slitting his wrists.

Her voice is quiet but high, and she sounds young. The prisoner doesn't respond. She talks to him about God and all of the good that there is in the world, probably not realizing that she's just making his decision to leave this place even easier.

I try to open my eyes again but it's a struggle so I give it more time. Flashes of what happened in the shower come back to me, sending shivers down my spine. For a second, I consider doing what that other poor bastard did, just end it all with one clean slice.

But then my thoughts return to Olive. No, she's worth fighting for. Even if she was the one who turned me in, I've got to stay strong for her. I've got to prove to her that I didn't do those horrible things they are accusing me of, if it's the last thing I do.

"He's not going to make it," a nurse with a deeper and lower voice says, walking right next to me. My heart sinks.

"No, he'll be okay. Those bruises will heal eventually," the younger nurse insists. She touches the sheet draped around my torso and I feel it get taut under her palm.

"I'm not talking about that."

"What do you mean then? The rape?" The last part she says so quietly, it's barely audible, as if the word itself is forbidden.

"No, that happens all too often," the older nurse says in a nonchalant sort of way that makes me sick to my stomach. "I just don't think he's going to make it through the trial."

"What do you mean?"

"Eh, he's too famous."

"It's not like he's an actor or a celebrity or something."

"He's a celebrity in these circles. His face has been all over the news and he was on the FBI's list."

A loud sound of metal hitting metal

interrupts their conversation, but only briefly.

"What does that matter?" the younger nurse asks.

"Everyone is talking about the four guys who did this to him. What do you think is going to happen to the one who puts a shank into him and watches him bleed out?"

The grotesqueness of the details makes me want to vomit but I can't seem to move a muscle.

My body is still too weak and tired. The only thing I can do is to put these images out of my mind by replacing them with something else.

I take a small breath and focus my mind on a place that's far away from here.

I see a little cottage overlooking the sea. The breeze is warm and there are palm trees swaying nearby. The cottage is freshly painted, white with blue shutters and a white-picket fence that Olive would love.

I see her in the garden, kneeling down next to a bushel of daisies that she has planted herself. Everyone loves roses but daisies are Olive's favorite. They are sunny and friendly and unassuming and yet breathtakingly beautiful just like she is.

The sun is setting somewhere over the horizon as I walk up to her and take her into my arms. She wipes the sweat off her brow with the back of her hand and gives me a kiss on the lips. Just then a little boy of about two with blonde hair and blue eyes runs out of the cottage. He is followed closely by a white and gray dog with blue eyes to match. They swirl around us filling the air with their contagious laughter and happiness.

13

OLIVE

WHEN I MAKE A CHOICE...

Ricky has provided me with more answers than I could've dreamed of but it's still not enough. Even after he leaves, I debate whether I should ask him if he would tell the FBI and tell them that he was with Nicholas that night. He was his alibi and that has to mean something, right?

Perhaps, but I suspect that it would only mean something if the FBI were actually after the truth instead of trying to make a case as good as possible.

Besides, Ricky was there right after committing a crime. I doubt that he would be too eager to come forward unless the situation was already going to trial or worse.

Ricky's answers provide context but still leave me grasping for more. Suddenly, I have even more questions than I had before. It takes me almost an hour to get home and when I finally do, I come to a rather dire realization.

If I want to free Nicholas, I'm going to have to figure out who killed both his old partner and his ex-girlfriend and not just that, I'm also going to have to find enough proof to convince the prosecutor that the cops are wrong.

At home, I make myself a cup of tea and grapple with what seems like an impossible task. If Ricky doesn't know who killed David, and hasn't figured it out in all of these years, how am I supposed to? And what about Owen's ex-girlfriend? He was so certain that Nicholas did it and now the FBI is, too. My heart sinks to the bottom of my stomach. Each breath becomes laborious.

I finish one cup of mint tea and quickly follow it up with another. The hours spent in the car have chilled my body to the bone and I'm having a harder time than usual warming myself up.

I search the cabinets for something yummy to eat. I go past the dry granola and the power bars and skip over the chocolate candy and sour lemon drops.

Then, at the back of the cupboard I find last year's marshmallows. They are thick and oversized, big enough to put on a stick to make s'mores. I impale one with a fork and turn on the lower right hand burner. I watch the marshmallow melt and get darker around the edges as I move it up and down to even out the heat distribution. When it's a nice shade of brown with edges that are almost black, I blow on it to cool it off and then bite into it.

I've never shared a marshmallow with Nicholas and I wonder about his technique. Does he wait for it to brown all over or is he one of those super patient people who will keep it just far enough from the flame to melt the inside without toasting the outside? The one time I've ever had one of those, it practically melted in my mouth. It was the most delicious thing I've ever had but as soon as I finished it, I also realized that I did not have the energy or the dedication to make them this way.

"What if I looked into his ex-girlfriend's murder?" I ask myself, biting into another marshmallow that's soft and chewy on the outside and hard and cold on the inside. "Maybe that would give me a glimpse into why the FBI is connecting those two crimes?"

I go into it knowing full well what it is that I have to do but not wanting to do it.

I HAVEN'T BEEN to my mother's house in a long time. Frankly, I thought that maybe I would just go through the rest of my life never seeing her again. A part of me was hoping I could, but another part gnawed at my conscience.

She is the woman who raised me and even though I know she could have done a better job and I blame her for the fact that she hadn't, I can't help but still find some love for her.

It's so easy for others to say to just cut out

the toxic people from your life, but it's a very difficult thing to do.

The people that get entrenched the deepest are those who are tied to your childhood. They are those who raised you and those who you cannot erase because that would mean erasing every part of who you used to be.

My mother is no different. She is selfish and self-absorbed and yet occasionally she gives me these glimpses of love and I allow myself to sustain life on them. It's not healthy and sometime in the future, I will finally commit to some therapy and force myself to examine everything that I have been burying deep inside. Today is not one of those days.

Today, I'm coming to her for answers. I need her help but I can't ask her for it directly.

She is the type of person who will take every advantage and if she knew that I needed her for something, she would make me pay dearly for that information, partly to get me back for abandoning her and partly just out of spite.

I show up without warning. If she's surprised, she doesn't let it show when she opens the door.

Instead, I walk right into the middle of the conversation with her telling me about the next door neighbor and how obsessed she is with her tree.

They had a friendly relationship up until now but apparently my mother's healthy tree somehow got in the way. The neighbor has decided that the tree is a hazard and needs to be taken down but my mother hired a tree doctor and confirmed that it is, in fact, healthy and should live for decades more. When the neighbor insisted that she take it down anyway, my mother fought back.

I wasn't aware of this argument but she quickly catches me up while insisting that I heat her up a frozen dinner of macaroni and cheese. We fall into our old traditions so easily that I have to physically stop myself from folding her laundry and putting it away while we talk.

"Listen, I need to talk to you about Owen's ex-girlfriend."

"Oh, you mean the one that Owen thinks your boyfriend killed."

I feel anger start to rise up to the surface, but I take a deep breath to keep it at bay.

"Why don't you tell me more about what happened in California?" she asks.

14

OLIVE

She thinks this question is going to take me by surprise but, of course, it doesn't.

I knew that she would never give me an answer free of charge, so to speak. If I want something from her, I have to give her something in return.

"I met my biological mother," I say sternly, looking straight into her eyes.

"So, I guess you know now," she says with a smirk. "And you're what, *mad* at me?"

"Not so much mad but disappointed. Why did you keep this from me?"

"I needed your respect. Kids need to respect their parents and there was no way you were going to listen to anything I said if you knew the truth."

I search her face for any inkling as to whether or not she is telling me the truth. Is she being serious?

"You lied to me about being my adoptive mother because you didn't think I would respect you?" I ask. "Don't you know that you get respect when you earn it?"

"Well, that's where I went wrong with you. I was always too lenient and that's why you turned out the way that you did."

I shake my head and look down at the pile of laundry on the edge of the bed. It's hard to tell whether it's clean or dirty and smelling it doesn't help matters.

"So, how is she? Is she everything you could have wanted?"

"She is...quite wonderful actually."

"Oh, yeah, then why the hell did she give you up?"

"She didn't. Her father took me away from her when she had an emergency C-section and she spent years looking for me. And he paid you a very generous amount to keep your mouth shut, didn't he?"

This conversation is going well off kilter but I can't help myself. Sometimes, the right thing has to be said even if it's at the wrong time.

"That is not what happened," my mother insists but the expression on her face says otherwise.

An emptiness comes into her eyes, the kind that's difficult if not impossible to blink away. She tries but instead I see a small tear form somewhere in the corner. So, there it is, huh. Perhaps she is human after all.

"You got Owen arrested, didn't you?" she says, clearing her throat and with one move erasing every last hope of humanity within her.

I don't know how much she knows but I have nothing to hide.

"He attacked me, pretty badly. He stalked me. Tried to rape me. Probably wanted to kill me."

My mom laughs and waves her hand as if I have just said the most unbelievable thing.

"Oh, please, you've always had such a flair for the dramatic."

There has never been a statement that

has been less true. Even as a kid, I hardly ever told stories, and made them up even more rarely. Tears come to my eyes but I push them away.

"Tell me about his girlfriend," I say, pressing my nails into my thigh to stop myself from crying.

"What do you want to know?"

"Anything. Everything."

"They were in love, or thought they were. Then they broke up. Or maybe she broke up with him. Then he heard that she was dating someone else, your Nicholas. He heard stories about him, about how dangerous and volatile he could be. He didn't want her to get hurt. He followed her a lot, trying to protect her. It didn't work, I guess."

The nonchalant way that she states these 'facts' send shivers up my spine. There is some truth in the story but she has reconstructed most of it in such a way that it's hard to tell what's true and what's false.

On the far end of the dresser, there's an extensive collection of pill bottles and Mom grabs one. Unscrewing the top, she dumps a few into her cupped palm. I want to stop her but I don't want to make this night even worse. She will just fight me on it and then refuse to tell me anything else. No, this is one battle I won't engage in tonight.

I watch her down the pills and wait for her to continue. But she doesn't.

"Is there anything else you can tell me?"

She shakes her head.

"Nicholas didn't do this."

"Owen thinks he did."

I shake my head.

"Is there anyone else who was there?"

Mom lifts her chin in the air and thinks about it for a moment.

"Well, I'm sure you've talked to Pink Eye already, right?"

I furrow my brow. When I ask her who that is, she just starts to laugh.

"C'mon, you must remember Pink Eye. He and Owen were best friends back then. He'd know more for sure and if he's not locked up somewhere, I'm sure he'll be the one to convince you that Nicholas is bad news."

"Pink Eye? That's his name?" I ask.

"Yep, pretty dumb, huh?" She smiles. "He

got pink eye when he was a kid and the name stuck somehow. They were really close once. Robbed a lot of people together, but then he just disappeared."

"What do you mean?" I ask.

"Don't know. I asked around a bit all of those years ago, but no one from that old neighborhood knows a thing. He wasn't even there that night that Owen got arrested."

I stare at her, thinking through everything that she's saying. I wonder if she even realizes the gravity of her own words.

If Pink Eye was Owen's best friend from back then and then suddenly he just took off, disappeared, maybe he was the one who killed Owen's girlfriend?

She reaches for a packet of potato chips and flips on the television.

"Are we done here?" she asks. "My show is starting soon."

"But I have so many more questions now," I protest.

"I don't care." She shakes her head, ushering me toward the door. "I'm done talking."

"Okay, okay, I'm going," I say, throwing my arms up. "One last thing, though."

She rolls her eyes but doesn't kick me out quite yet.

"Do you know where I could find Pink Eye?" I ask. "Or his real name?"

She stares at me for a while before she blinks. "No idea."

"No idea where I can find him or his real name?"

"Both," she says and shuts the door in my face.

15

OLIVE

WHEN I HELP HER...

The following morning, I accompany Sydney to a shop for her bridal dress. I've never been to one but have seen more than my share of them on television.

The boutique is spotless and outfitted in every possible color of creme. The floor is made of marble and there's a pedestal in the next room with a large three-panel mirror where the bride can stand and look at herself.

Under normal circumstances, this would be a joyous occasion to share with my best friend. But this day is covered in ominous clouds. Sydney is not getting married for the right reasons, in fact she's getting married for all of the wrong ones.

I've tried to talk to her about this before and I want to say something again but now is not the right time. She knows exactly how I feel and re-stating all of those things will just make her feel worse about herself.

No, now she needs me to be a friend and that's exactly what I intend to do. A tiny, size zero sales associate dressed in black, from head to toe, approaches us smiling from ear to ear with her pearly whites.

She asks Sydney a million different questions about the kind of dress she wants to get. I wait for her to waiver and hesitate but she comes right out and tells her she wants something with a mermaid cut that accentuates her hour-glass figure. The sales associate sweeps her over to their inventory against the wall and somehow peruses through the piles of identically colored dresses to pull out the ideal contenders.

While I wait for Sydney to get changed, I lose myself in research on my phone. My mother said that she had no idea what Pink Eye's real name was but someone has to, right? I go through Facebook and look at every person who Owen is friends with. Most of them don't have the privacy settings set up so it's easy for me to peruse through their friends list and look for any identifiable names.

When I get started, I think that I might actually stumble onto someone named Pink Eye but I quickly give up that notion. After Sydney comes out in one dress that makes her look so beautiful I practically tear up, I turn my attention back to the phone and start contacting every one of his friends with the same prewritten message.

Hi, my name is Olive Kernes and I'm Owen's sister. I am looking for an old friend of his who used to go by the name of Pink Eye. It's very important that I get in contact with him. I hope you can help me. Do you happen to know his real name? Or a current address and/or place of employment?

I write the message from my profile to make sure that they can confirm that I am indeed his sister and not some law enforcement officer.

When Sydney is on her fifth dress, I put

down my phone and give up on the fact that I will get a response this quickly. Not everyone is obsessed with social media, Olive, I say to myself but that doesn't mean you won't find him.

"I think I like this one the best," she says, straightening out the Vera Wang dress that hugs her body in just the right places, giving her the outline of a goddess.

"You look...amazing," I whisper, covering my mouth with my hand.

"Thank you," she mumbles.

The saleswoman looks for the tears that almost all brides get in their eyes when they find the perfect dress, but Sydney doesn't have any.

"Would you like to purchase it now?" she asks after a moment.

"Do you think I should bring my mom here first?" she asks me.

"Wouldn't she get upset that you were already here with me?" I ask with a shrug.

"She doesn't have to know."

The saleswoman and I exchange looks.

"So, you're going to go through all of this

again?" I ask for both of us. "Why didn't you just bring her here right from the start?"

"Eh, you know why." Sydney throws up her hand. "You know how she is. I wanted to decide on the dress in a normal, supportive environment and then fight her on it and ignore every negative thing that she says about it."

I shake my head and smile.

"Oh, you think that's funny?" she asks, also starting to laugh.

"Kind of. A little," I admit. "I guess the thing that I find the funniest is how fucked up our moms are."

That's when we both start to crack up. It might be the tiredness or the glass of champagne that's finally hitting us, but somehow the day feels like it has been saved just a little. Maybe it's not so bad after all, especially given that we have each other.

"So, what do you think I should do?" she asks me when we start on our second round.

She's still wearing her dress, though she's no longer standing on the pedestal.

"About what?" I ask.

"About my mom."

I look at her and lose myself in her bridal glow. Even though her groom is far from magical and their relationship is a house of cards, maybe there is some way that this dress can make up for everything.

"Don't bring her here," I say. "This moment is perfect. You found your ideal dress. You look beautiful in it and you love it. You're practically glowing, for crying out loud."

She laughs and twirls. The saleswoman runs over to take the glass away from her but there's no need. Sydney is practically walking on air and there's nothing that she can do that will bring her back down to earth.

If she brings her mother here then she will ruin everything and make Sydney feel like shit again. And she deserves a lot more than that. She deserves only the best and I hope that one day she will find a man who appreciates everything about her as much as I do.

"I love you, Olive," she says, throwing her arms around my shoulders.

"I love you, too, Sydney. Thank you so much for sharing this moment with me."

"I wouldn't have it any other way," she whispers into my ear. "Under any other circumstances, I'd probably raise the glass for you to find the same happiness as I have but I want to spare you the misery."

"Oh, c'mon, please don't say that." I pull her closer to me.

She puts her head on my shoulder and starts to sob. The saleswoman quickly swoops in and takes both glasses away from us so that I can use both of my hands to hold her.

"You're going to be okay, Sydney. And if you don't want to do this, you don't have to."

Instead of responding, she just continues to cry. I wish I could make things better but the more I talk the worse it gets.

Even though I don't convince her of what a terrible idea it is to marry James, she does agree not to sully the moment by bringing her mother here. After changing back into her clothes, she pulls out her wallet and puts the whole ten-thousand dollar dress on her credit card.

"Wow, you must have one hell of a credit limit," I joke.

"It's American Express," she says.

I furrow my brow, not sure what that's supposed to explain.

"There's no limit but you have to pay the whole balance at the end of the month," she explains. "Besides, Mom checks the bills so I'm sure that I'm going to hear about it early tomorrow morning."

Walking out of the bridal boutique, I get a notification that I have a new Facebook message. It's actually about the sixth one but I haven't had a chance to read them quite yet.

This one is from one of the first guys I contacted on Owen's friend list.

YEAH, *I know Pink Eye. Wow, what a blast from the past. His real name is Robert Bortham. I have no idea where he lives or what he's doing now.*

I STARE at the message in disbelief. My heart starts to race and I take a few deep breaths to calm down. I repeat his name over and over again until it's burned into my memory.

"Who are you, Robert Bortham?" I ask under my breath. "Who the hell are you?"

16

OLIVE

WHEN WE GO OUT TO LUNCH...

I don't tell Sydney about Pink Eye or much about what I have been doing to find out the truth about Nicholas. I want to, of course, but the timing has to be right.

Right now is no different. I invited her out on a celebratory lunch to commemorate her buying her wedding dress. This is the time to talk about wedding plans, their future and their hopes and dreams, not my boyfriend's murder charges.

But I can't seem to shake what I just found out. When she excuses herself to go to the bathroom, I grab my phone and start to look up every Robert Bortham in the area.

The name isn't that unusual but it's also

not that common. Most of the people that come up are the wrong age and a few live abroad. I thought that he would still be located in Massachusetts but there are no Robert Borthams in the state that even come close to being the right age.

Outside of the ones who are British expats living in Australia and Portugal, there is one profile that I keep coming back to. His age fits but I can't believe that this would actually be him.

I stare at the picture of a psychologist with a boyish grin in front of a wooden cabin. According to his profile, he is married with three kids, all under the age of five. Not sure as to what to do next, I take a screenshot of a closeup of his face and send it to my mom.

Could this be Pink Eye? I text her.

Before I can make up my mind about whether or not I should contact him directly, Sydney comes back and I toss my phone back into my purse. We finish the first round of drinks and quickly move on to the next. Our conversation drifts without any particular purpose even though there is something that I have been wanting to speak to her about.

The last time we spoke, she admitted some things to me about James and we just left it at that, but maybe that was wrong.

Maybe I should've pushed her further.

"So, how are things with James?" I ask, not wanting to come right out and ask if she's really going to marry him.

Sydney shakes her head.

"What about him cheating?" I ask.

"What about it?"

"Did you guys talk about it?"

"Yes, of course. He apologized," she says with a shrug.

I take a deep breath and look at her.

She runs her finger around the edge of her glass and avoids eye contact with me.

Then she takes a big gulp.

"If you don't want to talk about it—"

"I don't," she cuts me off.

We sit in silence for a long while. I don't know what else to say and I can't seem to let this go.

"I just don't understand why you need to do this. I'm sure that your mom will get over it."

"Really? Are you really sure about that?"

I shrug.

Well, no, I'm not entirely certain but she will just have to, right?

"My mom will blame me for him cheating on me," Sydney says, leaning back against the booth.

"Okay, that is really fucked up. But even if that does happen, so what? You deserve so much more than him."

Sydney shakes her head.

"You don't think so?"

"So, you would never forgive Nicholas if he cheated on you?" This time she does look up at me.

She peers directly into my eyes and I'm the one to look away first.

"I would never accept anyone treating me like that," I say, clenching my jaw. "I deserve better and it would be a deal breaker."

I try to imagine Nicholas doing something like that and I just can't.

I didn't want to say that but it's true. He is capable of incredible deception and he does live a life full of secrets, but when it comes to cheating, I know that he would never do that to me.

Sydney shakes her head and rolls her eyes.

"Is it not the same for you?" I ask.

"It's not so easy for me, Olive. Things in my life aren't just roses and chocolate. I have the real world to deal with."

I tilt my head to one side.

What is she talking about? No, this is about something more.

"What's going on, Sydney?"

She buries her head in her hands. I put my arm around her and she just shrugs it off. I do it again, and again she shrugs me off. When she finally comes up for air, her eyes are covered in tears.

"Mom said she would cut me out of her will if I don't marry him," she says. Her voice is weak and barely audible. "She won't leave me any of her money and she won't support me anymore."

I nod and put my hand on hers. I know that it probably doesn't seem like a big deal to most people who don't have family money flowing into their coffers every month, but Sydney relies on it. She lives off it and without it she will have to significantly cut back on her spending.

"It's going to be okay," I say. "You have a good job."

"That's the thing, though, I don't. I got fired."

"Well, that's okay, you have a good degree and experience. You'll be able to find another job."

But Sydney just shakes her head.

"Listen, you are just going through a tough time right now. But you can't marry him. He doesn't love you. And you can't just be with him because your mom likes him and will cut you off otherwise."

I regret my words as soon as I see the fire in her eyes. I don't regret what I said just the way that I have said it.

"You know what, Olive, you have some nerve," Sydney says, getting up from the booth and grabbing her purse. "Why don't we review all of the things *you* did for a little bit of money? You went all the way to Hawaii to meet some stranger and let him do who knows what to you—"

"It was all consensual," I interject.

"Yeah, yeah, whatever. So, you wouldn't have done it if he was old and ugly?"

"To tell you the truth, no, probably not."

"And what about your debt?"

"I would've tried to pay it off some other way."

"It doesn't matter!" she yells so loudly a waitress comes over and tries to calm her down. "Just remember that you did that for a little bit of money. Not the multiple *millions* that I stand to inherit."

"Sydney, I didn't—"

"Ma'am, I'm going to have to ask you to leave," the waitress says sternly. "You are disturbing the other diners."

"Fine, fine. I'm leaving," Sydney snaps and starts to walk away from me.

I'm about to follow her when the waitress reminds me that someone still has to pay the bill. I pull out my card and wait for it to process, hoping that I can catch up to her in time.

While we stand here, my phone vibrates and I glance at the screen. It's a message from my mom that says, *yep, that's him.*

The words ring in my head as I walk out

of the restaurant and run down the street. Sydney is leaning against the wall with her head in her hands. When I rush up to her, she opens her arms and pulls me in.

"I'm so sorry," I mumble.

"No, I'm the one who should be sorry. I shouldn't have said any of those things."

We hold each other for a few moments until she pulls away. Looking straight into my eyes, she says, "I'm pregnant."

17

OLIVE

WHEN I INVITE HER ON A TRIP...

Everything happens so quickly that it leaves my head spinning. My mom just confirmed that the guy up in Maine is Owen's old friend Pink Eye and Sydney just told me that she is pregnant.

Somehow, I manage to get her back to our apartment and we both change out of our street clothes into pjs. I put on the kettle for me and make her a fresh pot of coffee. Then we curl up on the couch together.

This time, I don't press her. Unlike at lunch, I give her space to open up to me. I know that she wants to talk to me, she just might not want to speak to me right at this moment.

Sydney opens an issue of Oprah magazine and leafs through the pages. I turn on my iPad and start to read my mom's latest release. I haven't read one of her books in a while and the story captivates me right from the beginning.

"Don't you want to know about it?" Sydney says in a huff, closing the magazine on her lap and turning toward me.

"Of course, I do. I just didn't want to push you."

"Well, push away."

"Okay, tell me everything."

Sydney takes a deep breath and starts at the beginning. She tells me about how hard she fell for him when they first met and how she thought he was the love of her life.

She loved sharing him with other women and men but when he cheated on her, it broke her heart.

They had strict rules about that kind of thing and have talked about it in detail. There was to be no cheating and no romantic or sexual talking or texting with anyone when the other person wasn't there.

And then the day after she caught him

and broke up with him, she found out she was pregnant.

"How far along are you?" I ask.

"Six weeks."

"What do you want to do?"

"I'm going to keep it."

I smile at her, in awe of her bravery.

Honestly, I don't know what I would do if I found myself in her situation. To say it would be a difficult decision would be a gross understatement.

"It was sort of around the time that I was talking to my mom on the phone and I casually joked about what would happen if we broke up," Sydney says. "And she just interrupted me and said that she would cut me off."

"Seriously?" I ask. "Just because she likes him so much?"

"Yes and no. It's more than that. She basically thinks I'm a fuck up and if James were to break up with me then it would be my fault."

"But what if you told her he cheated on you?"

"She's one of those old school women

who thinks that men cheat only if they aren't getting what they need at home."

"That's...disgusting," I mumble. "Sorry, I mean, I know she's your mom but that's awful."

Sydney shrugs. "Yeah, it's pretty shitty."

I don't say anything for a while, feeling her predicament.

"But you can't marry him and start a life with him if you don't love him," I say.

"First of all, people do it all the time. And who said I don't love him? The problem is that I do. And he's the father of my child. I have to try to make this work."

I nod.

"The other thing is the money. I can't argue with that. It's millions and millions of dollars, Olive. I can never make that much money and my child deserves to have access to it."

"Maybe she's bluffing?" I ask.

"Maybe, but I can't risk my whole future on that gamble," Sydney says. "I don't have a job and even if I were to get one, I don't want to raise this child alone. He or she deserves to know their father and I want their father to be in their life. If there's some chance that I can make it work with him, I can't throw it away."

The afternoon quickly turns into evening as we sit on the couch and talk like we haven't since I met Nicholas.

I tell her all about my life back in California and everything that has happened since then.

I fill her in on all of the details about Nicholas' arrest and the investigating that I have been doing to find out the truth and get him back to me.

As expected, Sydney is not so quick to believe in his innocence and plays the devil's advocate for a while. I actually appreciate it because it allows me to go through all of the theories of what might have happened, given what I know now.

Luckily, what she is receptive to is in helping me find out the truth.

"I guess we should go to Maine then and try to talk to this Robert Bortham," she says.

"Really? You want to come with me?" I ask, taken a bit by surprise.

"Of course, I'd love to go on a little road

trip and Maine is quite beautiful this time of year."

"If you like winter," I joke.

"The nature is breathtaking, you'll love it."

WE LEAVE THE FOLLOWING MORNING. I pack light with only one pair of leggings, two tops, a sweater, and a coat while Sydney brings a large suitcase that would have to go underneath the plane if she were flying.

"Are you planning on moving there?" I joke. She shrugs her shoulders.

"It's mainly just makeup and shoes. Boots take up a lot of space, you know."

"I do, that's why I'm wearing mine."

She throws her arm around my shoulder and gives me a peck on the cheek. "You know you love me."

"Of course, I do. What I don't love is your packing."

The drive from Boston to Bangor is just around four hours and we get there by early afternoon.

Surprisingly, his address wasn't that hard to find and required just a quick search through the white pages online.

The listing states that he is married to Allira Bortham and they have three kids together, and the kids' ages match his Facebook profile so the address must be correct.

"Is this really his house?" Sydney asks when we turn onto a long driveway heading toward the mansion at the far end of the property.

She searches the address on her phone and informs me that it has six bedrooms, six baths, a two-bedroom guest house, and sits on two-hundred acres.

The driveway is lined with towering pines and the occasional oak tree and the majority of the property is dotted with birches. The fresh snowfall makes the place look like a winter wonderland.

"This is so beautiful," Sydney mumbles.

"Are you sure we have the right place?" I ask.

She shows me the phone with the

address that I had found and memorized last night.

"I don't think I can do this," I say, gripping the steering wheel.

"C'mon, this is nothing."

"You say that but it's not true," I insist. My mouth feels parched.

"Olive, don't worry. You already went to see your biological mom and you did that all on your own. This is…"

"What?" I ask.

"This is…Pink Eye! You can't be intimidated to talk to Pink Eye."

I look at her and then we both burst out laughing.

18

OLIVE

WHEN I KNOCK ON THE DOOR...

After a little bit of prodding, I finally go up onto the porch and ring the doorbell. No one answers for a while. We wait. I ring again and again no one answers. Finally, I hear someone. I'm tempted to run back to the car, but Sydney blocks the exit.

"Can I help you?" a woman with a petite frame and thick red curls piled up on top of her head asks.

"I'm looking for Robert Bortham. Is he home?" I ask.

"Yes, he is. Are you one of his students?" she asks with a smile while holding a wet pan and a drying cloth.

I stare at her without saying a word. But luckily, Sydney comes to my rescue.

"No, we're not but we really need to speak to him."

"Sure, he's in his office. Do you want to follow me and I'll show you where it is?"

I've either been spending too much time in the city or with criminals but I am really taken aback by her hospitality.

The house is an old Victorian that has been completely remodeled and updated. The furniture is sleek and contemporary and is a perfect complement to the interior.

We walk on a polished wooden floor, down a beautiful foyer, and through the living room with enormous floor-to-ceiling windows that look out into forest behind the house.

Mrs. Bortham stops and knocks lightly on the door across from the open-concept kitchen with an enormous marble island in the middle.

"Honey?" she asks. "I'm sorry to interrupt but there's someone here to see you."

She opens the door just as Robert Bortham swivels around in his chair and faces us. Unlike many home offices, his desk is facing away from the door and looking out of the window at the birch trees.

As I stand debating whether or not I should bring up his past in front of his wife, she solves the dilemma for me by closing the door and politely disappearing back outside.

"How can I help you?" he asks, getting up from behind the chair. "I'm sorry, I don't remember you from class. Which one are you in again?"

"We're not your students," I say, clearing my throat. "I'm actually here to talk to you about something that happened a long time ago."

"Okay..." he says slowly, drawing out the word as he speaks.

He furrows his brow and waits for me to continue.

Enough already, Olive, I say to myself. Stop prolonging this anymore than necessary. Just say it already.

"My name is Olive Kernes," I mumble. Clearing my throat, I add, "Owen Kernes is my brother."

I search his face for an inkling of confirmation but his expression remains flat.

Did I make a mistake?

Is this the wrong person?

"You used to go by the name Pink Eye," I continue with newfound urgency. "You were very close friends with him back then."

He still doesn't react.

But he also doesn't look surprised.

"Please, I'm not the police, I just have some questions about something that happened to Owen's girlfriend...are you Pink Eye?"

The walls of his office are lined with bookcases and he runs his fingers along the spines of the books for a moment before descending onto the worn couch across from his desk.

"I haven't heard that name in many years," he says slowly.

"But you are Pink Eye?" Sydney asks.

He gives her a slight nod.

"I was...once."

When his wife comes in and brings us glasses of water and a bowl of cookies, I see his whole body tense up.

"My wife and I are very close, but she doesn't know anything about my old life," he explains. "And I'd like to keep it that way."

"Yes, of course," I agree.

"So, you were friends with my brother?" I ask.

"Yes. We were very close. But his arrest, the one he got all of that time for, that was a big wakeup call for me. That's when I stopped associating with all of our old friends and moved to Pennsylvania to my grandmother's house. That's when I really started focusing on school and ended up getting a PhD in psychology."

"And that's what you do now? Teach?" Sydney asks.

"Teach and do research. I also maintain a practice part-time, focusing on people dealing with post-traumatic stress."

I take a sip of my water and Sydney breaks off a little bit of the cookie.

"I have a small bar in here if you want to take the edge off," Robert says, walking over to a globe.

When he lifts the top, I see crystal bottles of various dark liquors. At first, I plan on saying no but it has been a long and stressful day with a lot of anticipation.

When he offers to pour me a bit of whiskey, I can't resist.

"So, you and Owen were close back then?"

"Yeah, I met him in the neighborhood and we were best friends for a few years. We did a lot of bad things together."

I swirl the golden brown liquid in my tumbler and then take a sip, enjoying the initial burn that levels out and spreads warmth throughout my body.

"Can you tell me about Owen's girlfriend, Nina?" I ask.

A smile appears on Robert's face.

"Nina was effervescent and so full of life. She was always laughing and making jokes. She seemed to walk on air."

I try to imagine the person that she knew as my brother. Was he kind and loving? Did prison turn him into the man I discovered him to be or was he always like that?

"Owen was obsessed with her. They were really in love at first, the way that teenagers

TELL ME TO LIE   151

are. They made plans. They wanted to get married. But then after a while, she got tired of him."

"What do you mean?" I ask.

"When they were dating and I wanted to hang out with Owen, we always had to hang out together. I liked Nina but I didn't like being a third wheel. But I was there when things started changing between them. At first, they were inseparable. They wouldn't go a day without seeing each other. But after a while, she would make these excuses as to why she couldn't hang out. He believed her at first, but then they started to grate on him..."

His voice trails off and he looks out of the window, lost in his memories.

"Was she cheating on him?" Sydney asks.

"No, I don't think she ever cheated on him even though I'm sure that Owen did. She just started to pull away and the further away she got, the more he wanted her closer."

"Was he possessive?" I ask.

He doesn't want to come out and say it but I can tell by his expression that that's exactly what he means.

"She ended up breaking up with him. But he still refused to take no for an answer. He called her incessantly and started following her. At first, she answered his calls and tried to explain but then she just started to ignore him. That made things...worse."

19
_____

OLIVE

I inhale deeply.

I start to have flashbacks to everything that Owen has put me through.

I take another breath, this time exhaling very slowly in an effort to steady my mind.

The behavior that Robert just described is, unfortunately, all too familiar to me.

"So what happened then?" I ask. He looks away and takes a few slow sips to finish his drink. When he is done, he looks at me.

"I have a feeling you know."

"Please tell me."

"She started seeing this guy Nicky we knew. And then they found her dead."

"Did Nicky kill her?" I ask, clenching my fists.

He doesn't know yet that he's talking about Nicholas and that's a good thing.

I want to know the truth.

I don't want him to sugarcoat anything on my behalf.

Robert shakes his head furiously. "Nicky? No, he didn't kill her."

"How do you know?" I ask.

"Soon after that, Owen got arrested for that convenience store shooting and I got really freaked out about everything that had been going on," Robert says, ignoring my question. "That's when I decided to just take off and move in with my grandma. Get as far away from that whole life as possible."

I nod. "That was probably a good idea."

"But I still think about Nina all the time. Especially now that I have a daughter who is getting a little bit older. What would I think if something like that happened to her when she was a teenager? I'd want answers, that's what."

"My boyfriend is a suspect in her death," I say slowly.

I don't mention that he has officially been arrested for the murder of someone else as well and they are just building a case against him to include Nina's case.

He furrows his brow and sits up in his seat. "Who is your boyfriend?"

"Nicholas Crawford. You knew him as Nicky C."

Robert shakes his head, muttering no, no, no under his breath.

"He didn't do it?" I ask.

Our eyes meet and he looks me square on without blinking. "Absolutely not."

"Who did?" I ask.

I feel my body starting to tremble because I suspect that I know the answer before he even says the words out loud.

"Owen," Robert says quietly.

"How do you know for sure?"

"He came to me and told me."

Now, it's my turn to sit back and absorb everything that he just said. "But why didn't you come forward? Why didn't you tell the cops?"

"I couldn't."

Because of some street code? I want to

yell. What about her parents? What about now? Don't you feel guilty?

"Why?" I whisper, as these thoughts flow through me like a river. Anger rises within me. I'm angry that there's a dark cloud hanging over Nicholas for something someone knows for sure he didn't do. But mostly, I'm angry at Owen for making me suspect Nicholas in that terrible crime.

"I couldn't come forward because I had robbed a bank that night and Owen knew it. He had proof. He was my alibi. So, when he came to my place covered in blood, I became his alibi."

WE DON'T STAY at Robert's house much longer. Our goodbye is brief, leaving a lot of things still unsaid.

I want to blame him for what happened back then.

I want to blame him for not coming forward, but who would?

Would I?

I can see that the guilt of what has happened still wears on him. Nina's parents don't know what happened to their daughter but he does and he could give them some solace except to do that would mean upending his own life and his own family.

Sydney and I talk about this on our way to our rental cabin.

"You know, you have to admit that this is still good news," she says as I turn down a narrow road in between sweeping snow-covered pine trees.

"Is this the right way?"

She checks her phone and nods.

"What do you mean?" I ask.

"Well, we now know for sure that Nicholas had nothing to do with that and we have an eyewitness to who did."

"Not exactly an eyewitness."

"Okay, whatever they would call it. Owen came to him covered in blood, that has to count for something."

"It does, of course. But only if he testifies in court and only *if* the FBI even believes him in the first place."

She takes a deep breath. "You know, you don't have to be so negative about this. You got a real breakthrough here. Why don't you accept it for what it is?"

I glance over at her.

I want to be as overjoyed as she is but somehow, she doesn't seem to see all the obstacles that are still in our way.

Like his wife, for one.

"Robert never even told his wife about this," I point out. "I'm not sure he will be willing to talk to the prosecutor."

"So, why did he tell you?"

"Because I already kind of knew. He wanted to get it off his chest. But that doesn't mean he's going to confess anything on record."

Sydney crosses her arms in a huff. "Does that mean he's going to just watch an innocent man go to prison for a crime he didn't commit?"

I shake my head.

I don't think he will go that far, but the thing is that Nicholas isn't even officially arrested for that crime.

He's just a suspect, but there are no formal charges.

I park in front of the cabin and we drag our suitcases through the poorly plowed snow.

When I get to the door, I worry that the code might not even work given the low quality of hospitality at the curb.

But I'm pleasantly surprised.

The cabin looks even nicer than it did on the picture and the owner even started the electric fireplace and the heater to warm the place up for us.

Solly looks concerned at first but then relaxes when I put him on the couch and let him curl up next to the fire.

"This is going to be a cozy place to spend the night," I say, putting my suitcase on the twin bed by the window.

Sydney is likewise impressed. After we take off our boots and change into our comfy clothes, Sydney makes hot chocolate.

"Thanks for coming," I say. "I don't think I could've done this on my own."

"You could have and you would have, but thank you." She gives me a wink.

"What do I do now?" I ask, staring absentmindedly at the flames dancing in front of me. "How do I convince the FBI that Nicholas didn't commit either of those crimes?"

"You probably have to make an appointment with the district attorney and go talk to him or her."

"I can do that?" I ask.

"Anyone can. Since you're his girlfriend, I'm sure that he'll meet with you and hear you out."

"Will he believe me?" I ask, playing with the tiny marshmallow in my cup.

"I have no idea," she says, placing her hand on my foot to show her support. "He's not still in Montana, is he?"

I shake my head.

"No, I don't think so. The murder happened in Massachusetts so they'll hold the trial there."

"Well, good, that way you won't have to travel far to go see the DA."

I nod. Yeah, what great news, I think to myself sarcastically.

"Okay, just put that out of your mind for

now. Let's relax a little bit, enjoy this hot cocoa, and try to laugh."

I glance over at her.

Her face is stoic.

She's being completely serious.

I give her a slight nod and say, "Okay, you tell me a joke first."

20

NICHOLAS

WHEN I'M ALONE...

I've never had much interest in music growing up. I've listened to my share of rap and rock 'n roll, just like any other teenager but I never really developed a taste for music.

It was always the words that I had focused on.

And now, sitting here and staring at these cinder block walls twenty-four hours a day, I try my best to remember even the most basic melodies to keep my mind occupied.

For some reason, the Christmas song, *The Little Drummer Boy,* comes to me and I run over the drum beat in my head. I know that it goes somewhere and doesn't just end after a few notes, but where I have no idea.

After I recovered somewhat in the infirmary, they transferred me to Massachusetts and put me into solitary confinement.

It's apparently for my own good since I'm somewhat of a celebrity and they are worried that I might not make it to trial.

But solitary isn't what it's cracked up to be, and it's not really cracked up to be much.

I'm entitled to one hour of outside time but I can only be out there when no one else is.

There are a few of us in solitary and the guards don't always take us outside. Someone's supposed to oversee the schedule, but it's not like we're in any position to complain.

When I first got here, I counted down the days by marking them on a piece of paper but then I got sick.

It was just a cold, but with my weakened immune system, it took me almost a week to recover and after that I didn't care about keeping track of days anymore.

Who gives a fuck anyway, right? I'm just another loser that the state has locked away.

All I can do in here is wait.

Wait and go through various stages of grief.

Last week all I felt was anger but now all I feel is apathy. It's like it doesn't matter what they're going to accuse me of next or what they'll do to me because I've already lost the one thing that I ever cared about; Olive.

But as soon as my thoughts come back to her, a spark that I didn't even know existed ignites somewhere in the back of my mind.

I have to fight to get out of here, if for no other reason than Olive.

I didn't do this.

I did a lot of bad things but I didn't kill David or Nina and I can't go down for murders I didn't commit.

But mostly, I can't let them put me away and have her believe them.

"Do you?" I ask. "Do you believe them, Olive?"

I wait for her to answer, but she doesn't.

"Please don't. Please remember who I was. Please believe me."

Tears start to well up in the back of my eyes but they emerge as anger as my fists collide with the pillow.

I take my anger out on it, flattening it beyond anything that's useful.

When I calm myself down, I sit down in the chair and write her another letter. I don't know where to send these and I doubt she'll ever read them but I have to write them anyway. I have to tell her the truth.

The guards go through my letters.

Nothing in prison is private.

And any smart inmate would never put any of their past crimes on paper, substantiating them into existence, but I'm not smart.

And I don't really care.

All I want is for Olive to get these letters somehow.

All I want is for her to know the truth about me.

I want her to know what I did and what I didn't do.

I want her to know that I didn't kill David and that I didn't kill Nina.

I don't know who did and I know that I

look like the most likely suspect but I want her to believe me anyway.

After I finish the letter, I put it on top of the stack of the other ones next to my bed and lie down again.

I don't know what time it is except that it must be day since the lights are still all on. That doesn't stop me from lying down, covering myself with a sheet and closing my eyes. Times of day don't matter much here. I am able to sleep anytime I want. The only problem is that I rarely can.

Sometime later, I open my eyes and nothing is different. The lights are still fluorescent and harsh and the time of day is still a mystery. It's sometime between lunch and dinner, but when? I have no idea.

Whenever it is, I'm not going outside again today.

They either forgot or don't care to take me there. I was looking forward to it even though it's just walking around a larger cement cage in circles all by myself as a guard watches me from the tower.

I want to spend all of my days in bed, but

it's hard and uncomfortable and it makes my back and neck ache.

Besides, I feel my muscles atrophying with each passing day and I can't let that happen. I get up and force myself to do push-ups.

I count to one-hundred and, by the time I get to the nineties, my form deteriorates.

Then I move on to jumping jacks.

Another hundred.

Sit-ups.

Another hundred.

I don't feel the tightness in my stomach like I usually do, so I keep going to two hundred.

Who cares, right? Anything to pass the time.

Despite the physical pain, my thoughts come back to Olive.

I lose myself in that cottage by the sea.

I lose myself in her beautiful hair and her soft body.

I imagine our child and our dog and those chickens she is afraid of but secretly wants.

How's Solly? I wonder.

Is he taking good care of her?

Will he get along well with our dog and baby?

Of course, he will.

He will even love playing with our chickens.

Why? Because it's my fucking imagination.

I run in place for a while, at first counting to one hundred and then giving up and just letting my mind drift.

I spend a lot time with Olive here but there's one thought that I always push away.

Today, it catches me by surprise and somehow penetrates my ideal world and throws acid all over it.

What if it was Olive?

What if I'm here all because of her?

21

OLIVE

WHEN I GET BACK HOME...

I t takes me a few days to schedule the
appointment with the district attorney in
charge of Nicholas' case. Perhaps, I should
first go to his lawyer, but I don't want the DA
to think that I'm biased, or any more biased
than I probably am.

I watch interviews with him online in
order to prepare myself but they don't make
me feel any better. He is combative and not
particularly kind. He's the shark that I guess
the state wants him to be. Still, I don't have
many options and I force myself to suck it up
and do what's right.

The security guard checks my
identification and I walk through the metal

detectors in the lobby without setting them off. When I get to the fifth floor, the doors open right out to a large room full of cubicles.

A part of me expects to see large windows and wood-paneling like they have on *Law and Order*, not an average corporate office. The administrative assistant in the front tells me where I can find the DA's office and I follow her instructions all the way to the back. There, another assistant tells me to wait until he's ready for me.

Just when I take out my phone, she tells me to go on in. I grab my purse and walk in.

The DA is on the phone but he points to the chair in front of his desk for me to sit down. The nameplate in front of me reads Connor Keenan. Dressed in a white shirt and tie, his suit jacket is hanging on the coat rack next to his desk. He is stern and short on the phone, which he hangs up without saying goodbye.

I extend my arm and introduce myself.

"Thank you for reaching out to me, Ms. Kernes. How can I help you?"

I start with the lines that I had
memorized earlier with Sydney.

It's better to go in there prepared rather
than just winging it, she advised me. So, we
worked out a script.

First, I tell him my name. Then I
reference the case and then I explain the
investigation that I conducted on my own
and give him all the pertinent details.

I talk for some time and the longer I talk,
the more uplifted I feel.

He wouldn't let me go on like this if he
wasn't actually listening. No, this must be
making sense to him. Maybe I can pull this
off, after all.

"Thank you for coming in, Ms. Kernes,"
Connor Keenan says. "I will take everything
you said under consideration."

Wait a second, what is going on here? I
furrow my brow and stare at him.

He meets my eyes and doesn't look away.
He's waiting for me to say something in
return.

"So...what's going to happen now?" I ask.

"I will take everything you said under

consideration," he says flatly. "But for now, I really need to get back to my work."

I continue to sit there for a few moments, but he goes on with his day as if I'm not here.

He opens one of the files in front of him and then turns his attention to the large computer screen to the left of his desk.

"So...I don't understand," I mumble

"Like I said, thank you for coming," he says. "Please leave."

He's so polite and cold, it takes me a moment to realize exactly what he's doing. He's blowing me off. He doesn't give a fuck about anything I just said.

"Are you not even going to consider it?" I ask.

"Of course, I will."

"But you didn't even take any notes."

"I took mental notes, please don't worry about it. We'll be in touch."

"But—" I start to say when his assistant bursts in and ushers me out of the room. "Wait, I still need to talk to you—"

"Mr. Keenan is a very busy man. He will get back to you at his earliest convenience," she says. "Now, please leave or we will be forced to call security."

I WALK OUT of the room dejected and disappointed. I thought that he would at least give me the decency of hearing me out. Now, I know that he only pretended to listen and was in fact waiting for me to stop talking so he could kick me out.

Uncertain as to what to do now, I hang my head low and walk past the cubicles. By the time I get to the elevator, a woman catches up to me.

"Olive Kernes?" she asks, trying to get a hold of her breathing. I nod.

"Okay, great, I need to talk to you," she mumbles, putting her hand on her chest.

"Take your time," I say.

Given her blunt haircut, immaculate and probably very expensive clothes and stilettos, I brace myself for some other barrage of disappointment.

"Sorry about that, I was just on the phone with an important client and I couldn't just hang up on him but I needed to catch up to you."

I shrug. I'm tempted to tell her to hurry up and tell me what it is she wants to tell me because I've had enough of this place for one day.

"Oh, I'm so sorry, my name is Meredith Clear. I'm a paralegal here and I have been following Nicholas Crawford's case very closely," she says.

This piques my attention.

"I've been watching all the crime shows and listening to the podcasts and the news reports along with reading all of the internal materials we have on the case," she continues.

"Oh, wow, that's..." I say. I'm about to say 'great,' but I'm not really sure if it is. She does work for the DA's office, after all.

She offers to buy me a cup of coffee downstairs and doesn't stop talking the whole way down.

She knows so much about his case she leaves my head spinning. She quotes information from different sources and then tells me which ones she believes and which ones are probably just speculations.

"Wait a second," I interrupt her after we get our coffees and sit down. "How did you get so involved? Are you working on the case for your boss?"

"Hell, no," she says, pushing her thick auburn hair from one side of her face to another. "I just know that Nicholas didn't do it."

22

OLIVE

WHEN WE TALK...

A wave of relief rushes over me. Through my own research, I got to the point where I am certain of this fact, but to hear someone else say it is hard to describe. It's like finally finding a kindred spirit, someone who is on your side when everyone else isn't.

"So, how are you working this case?"

"Well, I'm just a paralegal here but I love listening to true crime podcasts and watching all of those shows like Dateline and 20/20. Actually, a lot of people do since there's a big true crime community on the internet and his case has quite a following."

"You're doing all of this investigation on your own?" I ask.

She smiles and nods, taking a small sip of her latte. "That's what you have been doing though, right?"

"Yes, but he's my boyfriend. I have something invested in him getting out," I joke. This amuses her.

"Anyway, what I wanted to tell you is that there's DNA evidence available the state is refusing to test."

My mouth drops open.

"It's a re-election year and Keenan is afraid of finding evidence that doesn't fit their story. It will weaken their case, if not totally obliterate it."

"So, the DA is fine with putting an innocent man in prison just for the sake of his career?"

She stares at me as if I had just appeared out of thin air.

"Of course. Nicholas Crawford is one of the biggest cases of the year, he can't let it slip away. His opponents and enemies will never let him forget it."

I shake my head, feeling disgusted and

sick to my stomach.

"Besides, the FBI and the police know that Nicholas did commit other crimes, they just can't necessarily prove those."

I take a deep breath. This is difficult to argue with so I just let it go without either confirming or denying it.

"Do you know who the DNA might belong to?" I ask.

She shakes her head. She lays out everything she knows and I realize that I hold the pieces to the puzzle.

When I open my mouth, I hesitate.

Should I trust her, I wonder?

Do I tell her what I know?

My mind runs through the main eventualities.

Say I tell her and she actually is a spy for her boss, what then? Nothing.

Keenan will just get further confirmation of what I had already told him I knew. And if she thinks that Nicholas is innocent? Well, then I have even less to lose.

"I have to tell you something," I say. "I've talked to two people about this and, it's complicated, but once you hear me out, you will be even more convinced that Nicholas had nothing to do with what they're accusing him of."

Meredith listens carefully, containing her excitement as I launch from one story to another. At the end, she is practically jumping up and down and wrapping her arms around me.

"This is huge. Huge," she says over and over again.

"There's one other thing," I say at the end. "I think I know who did it."

She stares at me.

I take a deep breath. This is it.

If I tell her then there's no going back. Not that I want to, but a lingering feeling somewhere in the back of my mind remains. He was the person I thought of as my brother and someone who I thought would be in my life forever.

"Owen Kernes," I finally say. Meredith narrows her eyes. "He's my brother."

To my surprise, a big smile comes over her face.

"That's kind of who I thought it might be," she admits.

"Really?"

"A few of the podcast hosts mentioned him as a possible suspect. He did time in prison. He was in the neighborhood. And most importantly, he was Nina's ex-boyfriend."

I shrug, still finding it hard to believe that this can be true.

"The way he spoke about Nina, I always thought that he was in love with her. He was so angry at Nicholas. When he first told me that he thought that Nicholas killed her, I almost believed him. He was so certain."

"I'm so sorry," Meredith says, putting her hand on mine.

"But now, I know the obsession that he must've felt for her. At least, that's how he felt toward me. And if things hadn't gone my way back in California..." I let my voice drop off, unwilling to finish the thought.

"What is it?" she asks.

"I might have ended up just like Nina," I finally say after a few deep breaths.

Meredith doesn't know what happened so I tell her.

This isn't my first time relaying it and my

words feel almost on autopilot. After going over the story with the cops and the detectives and then with Nicholas and Sydney, you would think that they would be less painful to say.

Unfortunately, they're not.

That night still haunts me with flashbacks showing up at almost any time throwing me into a cold sweat.

"But how can we prove that it's actually him?" I ask. "Especially if the DA doesn't want to believe any of this?"

Meredith taps her hand on the table. "There is one thing we can do."

I wait for her to explain.

"If we can somehow get Owen's DNA and confirm that it's a match to the evidence they have at the crime lab then it would be something big to take to Keenan. Then he'll have to believe it."

"But doesn't the state have to authorize that?" I ask.

"I have a friend there who might be able to help," she says. "But the most important thing would be to get a sample Owen's DNA. Do you think you can do that?"

When Meredith lays out the plan of how I can get some of Owen's DNA, it sounds so simple.

All I would need is a discarded cup that he drank from or a few strands of hair. But the problem is that Owen is all the way back in California and locked up in jail.

As if that weren't complicated enough, there's also the interpersonal situation between us.

He had attacked me and I had promised myself that I would never talk to him again outside of a court proceeding.

"So, you're actually going to do this?" Sydney asks, walking into my room a few days later. I shrug, folding a pair of jeans into the suitcase spread out on my bed.

I have filled her in about the details and she even met Meredith who came over earlier and went over everything that I should do when I get there.

"I know that Meredith wants to help and I'm glad that someone at the DA's office is at least willing to listen, even if she's just a paralegal, but, Olive, this is *insane*."

"I know," I mumble.

"What if you can't get access to him? I mean, what if you have to talk to him through plexiglass?"

"I tried to find out what the situation was at the jail where he is being held but I couldn't get any details," I say.

"Exactly! So it might be a waste of your time."

"It might be but I have to try," I say. "What else can I do?"

"You can do what Nicholas' lawyer told you to do. Just not interfere with anything."

I clench my fists.

I went to speak to Nancy Leider, Nicholas' lawyer, and she acted just about as cool toward me as Conner Keenan.

She barely wanted to listen to what Robert Bortham and Ricky Trundell told me and I had to practically force her to write down their names and contact information so that she or someone at her office could follow up on those leads.

"I don't know what he's thinking about

using her, but she must be working for the prosecution. She doesn't give a fuck about Nicholas," I say through my teeth.

Sydney sits down on the bed next to me. She has, of course, heard all of this before.

"I just wish I could get a chance to see him," I mumble through the tears. "He's back here but they won't let me talk to him."

Sydney wraps her arms around me.

"Why won't they? Isn't he entitled to visitors? What are they trying to hide?"

These questions are rhetorical, of course, because I already know the answers.

Nancy Leider told me that they are holding him in solitary confinement and it's policy to not let prisoners in that situation have visitors.

"They said that he was badly attacked when he was with everyone else," Sydney says. "This is probably for his own good."

"But some inmates are in there for years. Do they never get visitors?" I ask.

"I think that's after they are convicted and there may be different rules for them, I don't know."

I take a deep quick breath and wipe my tears with the back of my hand.

I don't like thinking about this for long, otherwise I feel too helpless and overwhelmed.

"You see, this is exactly why I need to go to California and do this. If we can find out for sure if Owen is a match then it will make all of the pieces of the puzzle fit together."

"But you still don't know if Robert and Ricky will testify about what they saw," Sydney points out.

It's a long shot, I know. The district attorney wants Nicholas' head on a spike to make his career.

The two witnesses are more than a little bit reluctant because they have committed crimes of their own that they don't really want to get in trouble for.

And even if they were to come forward, it's unclear whether the jury will even believe them.

And that's exactly why I have to find out if the DNA is a match. It's the missing link. It's my only hope of proving that Nicholas had nothing to do with either of those murders.

23

OLIVE

WHEN I GO BACK...

The flight the following morning to Palm Springs International Airport is long but uneventful.

Josephine picks me up and helps me load my carry-on into her BMW. After a brief hug at the curb, we head over to her house, about a twenty minute ride.

She is, of course, my other reason for coming back here.

I was in such a bad place when I took off, I didn't know how to make things right.

I wanted to apologize so much and yet I couldn't find the words.

We've talked a few times since I got back

to Boston but every time I felt like there was this space between us that was only getting bigger and bigger with each conversation.

No matter how much I tried, I couldn't get through.

Josephine knows why I'm back here and she knows what I want to do. Since Owen was arrested for attacking me, his bail has been denied and he is awaiting trial.

I'm not entirely sure what will happen if, or rather *when,* he is convicted. He will probably get some time here and then he will have to serve the rest of his sentence in Massachusetts for fleeing the state and breaking the rules of his parole. The two states will probably have to decide where he will serve his sentence or maybe he will have to do them consecutively.

This is not what I want to talk to Josephine about though.

Instead, I want to apologize for not being open.

I want to thank her for opening her home and heart up to me.

I want to thank her for not turning me away when I first came to see her.

I want to thank her for introducing me to her husband and her children.

I want to thank her for never stopping looking for me. And mainly, I want to ask her if I can call her 'Mom.'

But as we drive up into the hills and I lose myself in the blueness of the sky and the warmth of the sun on my skin, I can't bring myself to say any of those things.

Instead, I just look at her and blink away a tear that threatens to run down my cheek.

———

LATER THAT EVENING, while we are drinking wine and laughing over Thai takeout, I finally tell her the whole story.

Her husband's brother is in town and they took all the kids to see a car race, leaving us alone in the house.

She gasps as I lay out everything that happened in Montana and how it felt to reconnect with Nicholas only to have him be torn away from me so abruptly.

She listens with her hand over her mouth as I tell her about going to see his mother and then Ricky and then my mother and taking the trip to Maine and finding Pink Eye, a recovered gangbanger living the life of a psychology professor and family man.

"This is one hell of a story, Olive," she says, opening another bottle of wine. I take a bite of a cracker, nodding my head.

"And you should know," I add.

"Have you ever thought about writing it down?" she asks.

"Writing? I don't know. I love to read novels but I don't know if I could write one."

"Many writers won't agree with me but I believe anyone can learn to write."

"Really?"

She nods.

"It's all about paying attention to details. The events and the plot points are one thing but what makes someone a writer is how they tell the story. You and I would tell the story in two completely different ways because the details that I would pay attention to and include are different from those you would include."

I tilt my head to one side, not really understanding what she's getting at.

Aren't all the details the same?

Like events in a sequence?

When I ask her about it, she laughs and shakes her head.

"No, not at all. Even the way you told me the story of what happened since you left my house, you included all of these descriptions about what you went through and how you felt about everything that was going on. You described what the motel looked like where you found Solly. You practically showed me the forest where Nicholas was camping and the way the water glistened in the sunlight."

I sit back against the upholstered chair.

Is she really serious or had she just had too much to drink?

"All of those things tell me that you have the mind to be a really good writer. And what's more, you have the perfect story to tell."

I bite the inside of my lip, thinking over what she had just said. She knows most of what happened now, except what occurred before.

She doesn't know how I met Nicholas; the

debt, the obligation, the promise to spend a year with him.

All of that seems like it happened a million years ago and yet just yesterday at the same time.

"Anyway, I don't want to pressure you, of course. I just wanted to encourage you to think about it. Writing is really, really hard but it gives you this enormous sense of purpose and accomplishment. You create a world and these people who didn't exist before and you bring them all into existence."

"But that's just with novels, not a memoir, right?" I ask.

"You would think so but no, it's the same with all writing. With a memoir, you are somewhat limited to facts and things that actually happened but, like I said before, two different people will have two different experiences of what happened because of how they view the world and themselves. Their stories will inevitably be different. So, in writing a memoir or a true story, you would have to do the same thing as you do in fiction. You have to create the character who experienced those struggles. It may have been you at one time, but it's likely not the you that you are today."

24

OLIVE

WHEN I GO TO SEE HIM...

Josephine drives me to the jail where Owen is being held. It's a nondescript looking building that looks more like an office or some sort of administrative structure than a jail. There's no barbed wire or guards with guns like the ones guarding the prison where I picked Owen up.

"Olive, I know that you are doing this for the right reasons but if you feel afraid, more afraid than you do now, or like you're in danger, then don't do it. It's not worth it," she says.

I give her a nod and a brave smile. Josephine is saying that to be encouraging and to give me permission to fail but I can't give myself that permission. If this doesn't work or if I am too fearful of facing Owen again, even in this protective environment, then Nicholas is going to go away for a very long time. No, whatever fears I have, I have to put them aside.

After I get out of her car, I give her a wave and promise to text as soon as I'm done so that she can come and pick me up.

I walk up to the guard behind a thick wall of plexiglass and tell him my reason before being here. He asks for my identification and then lets me walk through the metal detector.

To prepare for this visit, I've read through all of the requirements and scheduled the appointment yesterday as stated. I look down at my phone and check the time.

Visitor check-in begins twenty minutes before the scheduled visit time. Check-in is terminated ten minutes before the scheduled visit time and each visit is scheduled to be forty-five minutes in duration.

They have a cubby system for leaving cell phones and I check one out and pay the one-dollar fee to use it.

The guard shows me to the bench

where other women are seated. I am the only one here without a child or a baby in tow.

I think back to Josephine's children in her beautiful house overlooking the valley and the crammed apartments that these children probably live in and my heart breaks for them.

How is it that some people have so much while others have so little?

Without my phone to entertain me, time passes like molasses. I arrived right on time and I should only wait twenty minutes but it feels like it has been hours.

Finally, they show all of us into a large room with round tables and chairs bolted to the floor. There are small windows near the ceiling along each of the four walls but otherwise it looks a lot like the cafeteria where I ate lunch for four years at my pubic high school.

The inmates are already sitting at various tables, and I scan the room for Owen. Initially, there's a rush of excitement as the children run into their fathers' arms.

The guards watch carefully as we are only

allowed a small hug and a peck on the cheek, no excessive displays of affection.

That's not going to be an issue in my case.

I spot him sitting at the far table, near the entrance where he probably came through. His head is hanging low but he is searching the room with his eyes, eventually laser pointing onto mine.

I relax my clenched fists and put my chin in the air. I will not show him that I'm afraid. I will not show him that I'm intimidated.

Owen doesn't say a word when I walk up to him.

Suddenly, there are more lines on his face and his skin has a yellow tint to it, making it look sallow and tired.

"Thanks for meeting me," I say, sitting down across the table from him.

Out of the corner of my eye, I see a vending machine full of chocolate bars and chips and a huge plastic container of drinking water with small cups underneath.

Unlike the snacks, the water is free. The majority of the inmates are already stuffing their faces with one thing or another, but

Owen simply folds his hands in front of him and interlocks his fingers.

"What do you want?" he asks.

There's hostility in his voice.

I'm tempted to bite my lower lip but I don't. I knew that this wasn't going to be easy but I can't let him see me waiver.

"I wanted to talk to you about what happened," I say after a moment.

"Oh, yeah? Why is that?" His eyes narrow from anger.

I was hoping that he would be a lot more receptive to seeing me again, especially since it's a surprise, but now I realize that I have to make an effort to get through to him.

Right now, he is all ice.

But what we once had was a real relationship.

If I want him to relax and to get through to him, I can't be ice myself. I need to be vulnerable.

I glance down at the table and then slowly bring my eyes up to his. For a moment, I see the man I used to love like a brother and a friend.

"I just want to understand what

happened," I say after a moment. "How things went so wrong."

He shakes his head.

"You don't want to tell me?"

"What do you want to know?"

"Why...Why did you...why did you follow me and attack me?" I ask.

His eyes focus on mine and I see a tenderness there that I hadn't seen in a long time. But then he blinks, and it vanishes.

"I have no idea what you're talking about, Olive," he says.

His voice is dead and stoic.

"Why are you being like this?" I mumble.

"Do you think I'm stupid?"

"No."

"Do you think I'm an idiot?"

"No."

"Then why do you fucking treat me like I am?"

"What are you talking about?" I ask.

"I know what you're doing here, Olive. I'm not a fucking moron!"

My blood runs cold.

Shivers race down my spine as every muscle within me freezes.

He knows why I'm here?

How?

"Everything we say is being recorded. I'm not going to talk to you about what happened or didn't happen so you can make your shitty case against me better. You know what you did, Olive. You know that everything in that police report is a lie. You and I both know that."

The first breath is the hardest but once the air fills my lungs, the others come much faster and smoother. He was so confident and self-assured that he scared me when he said he knew why I was here. But now that I know he thinks that it's all about his attack, I have the upper hand.

"We don't have to talk about that," I say quietly, pretending to give him ground.

"What do you want to talk about then?"

"Us."

He narrows his eyes, trying to read me.

I relax my face and sit back.

I have nothing to hide because in reality I do want to talk about us.

"What happened to us?" I ask. "I really cared about you as my brother. All of those letters you wrote to me in prison, were they just lies?"

His shoulders slope down as he adjusts his seat. Talk to me, I say silently to myself over and over again. Just talk to me.

"Of course not. Everything I said was nothing but the truth."

"What about your plans for when you got out? When we got to California, you just seemed to let them go."

He shrugs.

"Doesn't matter now, huh?"

"I wouldn't say that."

"I broke my parole."

"So, you'll do a little more time but then you'll get out and you'll still have to figure out what it is that you want to do with yourself."

He rubs his temple with his index fingers. Then he brushes his hands through his hair and looks at me. This is the Owen I once loved. The one I thought I could talk to. The one I thought I understood.

"I'm going to get something to drink, you want anything?" I ask.

"No thanks."

My throat clenches up but I don't let it

show. I walk over to the water station and pour myself a little cup.

I didn't wait long enough.

I should've waited longer.

That way we could've talked more and his mouth would have gotten drier.

But it's too late now.

Shit.

Shit.

Shit.

"Actually, yes, can you pour one?" Owen yells over at me.

My heart skips a beat and my hands start to shake as I open the spigot and watch the water fill up the flimsy paper cup.

"Why are you here, Olive?" Owen asks when I hand it to him.

I watch him bring it to his lips and take it all down in one long gulp.

"I don't know," I say quietly, looking away from him. "There was a time when I thought you were my best friend and I guess I miss that. More than I'd care to admit."

Owen smiles out of the corner of his mouth.

"I've missed you, too," he says.

The guard makes an announcement that we all have one minute left. As I stare into his eyes, I don't know what else to say to him. A part of me does miss him. Even after everything that he has done and put me through, I can't help but mourn the man that I used to think he was.

When a guard approaches us, Owen rises to his feet. "Will you visit me again?" he asks.

"Yes," I lie.

He opens his arms and I force myself to make a move closer to him and let him embrace me.

I feel his heartbeat through his jail-issued uniform and I wonder at how normal it sounds, almost as if it belongs to a regular person.

After he pulls away, I wait for him to walk away so that I can take his cup.

But much to my shock and surprise, he wraps his fingers around the cup and takes it with him.

Unable to stop him or do much of anything, I start to exist in suspended animation.

I want to run after him, tackle him, and

take that cup from his fist but I know that the guards would stop me and never let me take it.

I wish more than anything that I could turn back time but instead I'm simply forced to stand here impotently and watch as Nicholas' fate is sealed away for good.

But then, a glimmer of hope!

Before he walks out of the door, Owen tosses the cup into the garbage can near the vending machine.

"Do you mind if I get some M&M's before I go?" I turn to the guard standing near my table. "I haven't had anything to eat today."

"Hurry up," he mumbles and walks over to another table with a screaming toddler who doesn't understand why his daddy has to leave.

I stick four quarters into the machine and press the numbers for the peanut ones.

Once I retrieve it from the bottom compartment, I rip it open at the top and toss the ripped piece into the garbage can next to Owen's cup.

After a quick glance at the room, I grab his discarded cup, careful not to touch the rim, and bury it in the arm of my oversized sweater.

With both of my hands showing, I pour some M&M's into my palm and walk out of the visiting area.

THE RESULTS...

Walking around Boston Common on my daily two-mile walk, I zip up my jacket all of the way to the top to try to keep the wind from chilling me to the bone.

It's hard to imagine that only last week, I was submerged in the warm turquoise water of my mother's pool watching the palm trees sway in the breeze.

I glance down at my phone at what feels like the fiftieth time today.

I'm expecting a call from Meredith with the news about the DNA test. I had sent the cup to them overnight in a Ziploc bag and it has now been almost ten days.

With official investigations, it can take a

year or more but Meredith has assured me that we can get the results in less than two weeks.

These are, of course, not official results.

She has a friend at the lab who has access to all of the samples that have been collected.

There are blood samples from the motel room where Nina went missing (her body has never been found) and there are samples from the scene where David was found.

Of course, it is highly illegal to mess with the data collected from crime scenes but Meredith assures me that her friend can use a small amount just to run the comparison test and leave the rest to be tested by an official decree.

I pick up the pace as I pray that he finds a match. In addition to being negative, the results can also be inconclusive and those will pretty much leave us exactly where we are right now.

The only hope that Nicholas has is if the DNA comes back a match to Owen.

My phone starts to vibrate and I answer even before it starts to ring. "Meredith?" I say.

There's a long pause.

This isn't good.

I shake my head and say her name again.

"It's a match!" she yells. "He did it! Owen killed both of them!"

I start to jump up and down, beaming and smiling from ear to ear.

I keep asking her if she's sure and not believing her when she says she is. She's still at work and won't be able to come over until the evening.

I run back home, excited to tell Sydney but she's not there either.

It takes me almost half an hour to calm down and as soon as Josephine answers the phone, my excitement explodes out of me.

"Oh my God," she says. "I can't believe he killed both of them. *You* are so lucky."

I pause. She's right. I hadn't thought about it like this before but Josephine is absolutely correct about Owen.

He killed Nina and David and he tried to rape me. If he had succeeded, he probably would've tried to kill me, too.

Goose bumps run up and down my arms and I rub them trying to make them go away.

We talk for a while and celebrate but

then Josephine has to go and wanting to have someone else to talk to, I call Meredith back and ask about the next step in the process.

"The thing is that now we have to tell the district attorney," Meredith says.

"Do you think it's going to be hard?" I ask.

"It's not going to be easy," she says with a sigh. "The thing is that I can't tell him that we already did the test because then my lab tech and I will definitely get fired and possibly face criminal charges for tampering with evidence."

Wow, I had no idea that what we did was that illegal.

"So, what do we do?"

"We have to somehow convince them to run the DNA without telling them what we know," Meredith says.

My mouth drops open.

I was certain that if we got the DNA match, we could share it with the world.

And now? Now, we have to keep it secret?

"That's not what you told me before," I say quietly.

She doesn't respond.

"I know, I'm really sorry. But we

tampered with evidence. We can't let anyone know, otherwise they're going to press charges. The only way to do it is to just try to convince the DA that Owen is the right guy."

She keeps repeating herself over and over again as if that's somehow going to change her story.

I let out a long sigh and watch my breath as it collides with the cold air and makes a large pouf as if it were made of smoke.

THE FOLLOWING MORNING, I go back to Nancy Leider's office. She's Nicholas' lawyer and this time, I'm going to make her listen.

I didn't fight hard enough for him before but now that I know the truth and I know that he is one hundred percent innocent, I have to make her understand.

Her assistant shows me into her office and brings me a cup of tea with an assortment of tea bags.

The office is plush and comfortable with thick carpeting, a luxurious upholstered sofa, the color of wheat, and a glass desk with very few things on it.

In fact, the office itself doesn't really look like it belongs to an attorney at all.

There's even a big faux sheepskin rug on the floor that I can't help but touch.

"Thank you for waiting," Nancy says, dropping her iPad on the table and folding her arms across her chest before asking me what she can do for me.

I hope that she's not just being polite but will actually listen to what I have to say this time.

I remind her that I'm Nicholas' girlfriend once again and start to review what I learned from Ricky Trundell and Robert Bortham when she interrupts me.

"You've already told me all of that before," she says.

"I know but I just wanted to go over it again in case you didn't hear me right before."

"I always hear everything right."

"Well, in case you forgot—" I start to say but she cuts me off again before proceeding to review all of the facts that I learned from both of them in a much more succinct and detailed way than I could've ever explained.

"What is it that you *really* came here to tell me?" Nancy asks, turning on the large computer screen on her desk and pulling out the wireless keyboard.

"If I tell you this, can you promise not to tell anyone?" I ask. She narrows her eyes.

"I can only do that if I am officially your attorney."

What is she doing? Is this some sort of ploy to get me to pay her?

"I don't have much money," I say.

She slides open the drawer in her desk and pulls out a single sheet of paper. I glance over it and it's a very basic agreement saying that she will be acting as my attorney and everything that happens between us will be privileged information.

"Sign this and pay me one dollar and I will never reveal anything you tell me without your permission."

I take a deep breath and write my name on the line. After I pay her in quarters, the only cash I have on hand, I tell her everything that happened.

"What you all did is a very serious crime," she says with a long sigh. "But I can't say that it doesn't give me some peace of mind knowing that I'm actually representing an innocent man."

A wave of relief rushes over me.

Finally, someone believes me!

"Okay, let me think about how we can approach this matter in the most delicate way possible and I'll be in touch."

"Thank you! Thank you so much!" I say, grabbing my purse.

"By the way," she stops me by the door. "If you have any interest in seeing Nicholas, they have just transferred him to Boston."

26

NICHOLAS

WHEN THEY TAKE ME TO A NEW PLACE...

P risons are the same and different. The location changes. Along with the people and some of the rules but the lack of freedom remains.

Some prisons are better than others mainly as a result of relationships. You meet some people you connect with, you make friends, and then you have to move. At least, that's what my new friend here in Massachusetts told me.

He's nice enough and he likes to talk. I like to listen so we're a good match. He's also not violent, which I appreciate since the last thing I want is to end up in solitary again.

My bruises have pretty much healed on

the outside, leaving me just with remnants of panic and sheer terror that comes out of absolutely nowhere and overtakes my body without my control.

I haven't felt this way since I was a child and had night terrors. Some people say that they happen to children just out of the blue. But mine didn't.

They were a result of my uncle and other scary men in my so-called family who not only didn't protect me but actually hurt me. But that's another story for another time.

That's the thing about being cooped up all day. You start to let your mind wander and the place it typically lands is somewhere pretty dark and inhospitable.

Today, I have a meeting with my lawyer.

She comes to visit me and nods compassionately as she brings one slice of bad news after another. It has been like this over the last seven visits, and today will be no different.

Honestly, if I could save her a trip and just read her emails, I'd appreciate it. That way I don't have to put on a brave face and pretend that what she's telling me is alright.

"Thanks for seeing me on such short notice," she says, sitting across from me.

We are separated by inches of plexiglass and holding ancient receivers to our ears so we can hear each other.

"Not like I have a busy schedule nowadays," I say with a shrug.

"I have some good news for you."

I raise one eyebrow.

"It's about Olive...your girlfriend." My heart tightens at the sound of her name.

"Ex-girlfriend," I correct her.

"I know that you have had your doubts about whether or not she possibly was the one who called the FBI."

I shrug, trying to pretend that I don't care.

"She didn't do it," Nancy says, shaking her head.

I narrow my eyes, not sure if I should believe her.

"If they found her by following her, that I don't know but she did her best to get to you without being seen."

"How do you know?" I ask, still skeptical.

"Let me tell you a little story," Nancy says.

As I listen to everything that Olive has

done ever since I got arrested, tears come to my eyes.

At first, I think that Nancy is making things up even though in her profession that's a very dangerous thing to do.

But after a few moments, I know that what she's saying is the utter truth.

She finishes by telling me about how Olive got Owen's DNA and confirmed that it was actually he who killed both of them. When I hear that part, I worry for a second that our conversation might be recorded and someone might use this as information against her.

"She really did all of that?" I ask, wiping away tears with the back of my hand.

Nancy nods and goes into her plan for getting the district attorney on board to do the DNA testing.

According to her, it will still be an uphill battle but she's on good terms with him and she hopes that handing them Owen, a convicted criminal, on a silver platter would be enough for them to let me go.

But it's still not a done deal.

I SPEND the next few days floating on a cloud. People get into fights around me.

They throw curse words and punches but nothing touches me. The only thing I think about is Olive. She didn't turn me in and she has been fighting to get me out of this Godforsaken place the whole time I have been in here.

She found out more than I ever thought was possible. She talked to Ricky and Pink Eye and so many other people from a world I thought I had left long ago. She even talked to my mother.

Olive is coming to visit me today and I have been counting down the minutes until I see her again. I won't be able to touch her or to even smell her but I will be able to see her and for now, that's enough.

It's finally time. A guard walks me down the long hallway. My standard-issued rubber shoes make a loud scratching sound as they hit against the linoleum. When the door opens, I see her. Her face lights up and she smiles. I practically rush over to get to the phone so that I can hear her voice.

"You're here," I whisper.

"I'm here." She nods.

Her hair falls a little bit into her face and she brushes it away. Our eyes meet and I see a tear in the corner of hers.

"It's okay, everything is going to be fine," I whisper.

I have no way of knowing that, but it's a good thought and right now I just want to think good thoughts.

"Thank you so much for doing everything you've been doing to help me. Nancy just filled me in," I say, putting my hand on the glass, wanting more than anything to touch her. "You really didn't have to, but I appreciate it so much."

"It was Owen all along," she says quietly. "He killed your partner and he killed his girlfriend."

I nod.

Looking back, it totally makes sense. That's why he was always accusing me of it. That's why he was upset with me being around her.

He wanted me to take the fall for his crime and here I am standing at the cliff.

Olive puts her hand up to the glass matching the outline of mine. But then she hangs her head and pulls away.

"What's wrong?" I ask. She doesn't respond so I ask again.

"Meredith got fired," she says quietly. I have no idea who that is.

"She's the paralegal at the district attorney's office who was helping me with the case. She knew everything about it and she believed that you were innocent."

"I'm so sorry," I say.

"And Robert, I mean Pink Eye, is refusing to cooperate. He told me one thing but now he's retracting his story. And without him and without the DA testing that DNA evidence..." Her voice trails off.

"Don't cry," I say. "Please don't cry."

But tears start to flow down her face. She wipes them off just as new ones arrive. After a few moments, she gives up and just lets them run.

"It's going to be okay, Olive," I say over and over again, trying to calm her down.

It's a lie. We both know it but what else is there to say?

What else is there to do but stay in this moment for as long as possible and hope against hope that tomorrow might be different?

27

OLIVE

WHEN I SEE HIM AGAIN...

Seeing Nicholas again after all of that time was supposed to be a joyous occasion. I wanted to celebrate the fact that I found out the truth about who killed those people, and in the process proved that Nicholas was innocent.

But then Meredith called. Keenan was refusing to budge on the whole testing the DNA issue and he was aggravated by how much she was advocating for Nicholas. It got so bad that he actually fired her.

At first, I thought that maybe he somehow found out about the DNA testing but luckily, she kept that to herself. Had she not, she would probably be facing criminal charges now, as well.

With her gone, I turn to Nancy for advice but she doesn't have any. She keeps promising to put pressure on the DA's office but so far that hasn't yielded many results.

I didn't want to tell Nicholas about any of this, of course.

I wanted to just enjoy our hour together. But I couldn't keep it to myself.

I saw how happy he was when he saw me and I was, of course, happy to see him, too, but I didn't want him to believe that everything was fine when it wasn't. And when I left, I saw the broken pieces of the man that I love.

There must be something else I can do to help.

That's why I'm here.

A long time ago, two police officers came to our door asking questions about a man who was last seen in my apartment building and who later was found dead.

He'd attacked me and tried to kidnap me but we couldn't tell the police the truth so we lied.

We lied.

And then we lied some more.

I walk up the steps of the precinct where I found out he works. The officer at the front desk looks up at me and I ask him where I can find Officer Dockery.

"Can you tell me what this is about?" he asks without changing the expression on his face.

"It's kind of personal," I say. "Is he working tonight?"

"Give me a second to make a call," he says, showing me to the chairs at the far end of the wall.

A few moments later, he hangs up and tells me to go down the hallway and through the double doors.

I do as he says but instead of Officer Dockery, his partner greets me and shakes my hand.

His name is Benjamin Inglese and he was also there that night.

After a few pleasantries and casual mentions of the weather, he asks me why I'm looking for Dockery. I'm here because he used to be good friends with Nicholas back when they were friends and their lives took different paths. But looking into Officer Inglese's earnest eyes right now, I decide to go on a whim and tell him about Nicholas' situation and how we could prove his innocence and another man's guilt if only the prosecutor got off his ass and did his job.

Officer Inglese listens and nods and then looks away briefly. What is going on here? I think to myself. Why is he acting like this?

"So is Officer Dockery here?" I ask. "I know that he and Nicholas were really close and I thought that maybe there was something he could do."

Officer Inglese shakes his head and looks down at the floor. "There's nothing he can do," he finally says.

"Why? What do you mean?"

"Dockery is dead," he adds quietly. I stare at him, not quite processing what he has just told me.

"He was shot and killed about two weeks ago."

"I'm so sorry," I whisper.

"Are you, *really*?" His eyes flash in anger.

"Yes, of course."

"Yeah, I wonder about that."

"What do you mean?" I ask, sitting back in the chair.

"Well, he was still hard at work on the case of the man who went missing from your apartment, remember him?" he asks. Shivers run down my spine.

Of course, I remember. How could I ever forget?

"I'm not sure what you're getting at," I say after a moment.

"My partner had that case in the trunk of his car when he was killed and his car was set on fire. You wouldn't know anything about that, would you?"

I shake my head. "Are you sure?" he asks.

"He suspected that something bad happened to that guy in your apartment and you and your boyfriend and brother covered it up."

"No, that's not what happened," I lie through my teeth. I look him straight in the eye and refuse to look away.

"Inglese, what are you doing?" Another cop approaches us.

I glance down at my hand and hide it

under my thigh as soon as I see how much it's shaking.

"I'm sorry," the cop says to me. "He is still quite distraught over what happened to Dockery but he, along with everyone else here, knows that he was shot by a stupid fifteen-year-old out on a joy ride who then set his car on fire to cover up the evidence."

I let out a sigh of relief.

"I am really sorry for your loss," I say to both Officer Inglese and the other cop. Only the cop whose name I don't know acknowledges my statement with a nod.

I hold my breath when I get up to leave. I shouldn't have ever come here but how could I have known?

28

OLIVE

WHEN NOTHING MAKES SENSE...

The following week, I go back to see Nicholas. I don't make an appointment, but I know that it's during visiting hours and I hope that the guard tells him I'm waiting.

It takes me longer than usual to get through the line of visitors and I go through two hand checks in addition to walking through the metal detector.

Once I'm finally in the waiting room about to go into the visitor area, a guard walks up to me.

"I'm sorry but Nicholas Crawford isn't available at the moment."

"What does that mean? Did he get in

trouble? Did something happen?" I begin to panic.

Ever since I got back from California, I seemed to have one blow after another.

I immediately think the worst.

"I am sorry, but I can't give you any more information at this time," the guard says.

I look at him but also through him, somewhere far away behind him.

I sit here on the cold metal chair for a long time.

It's only when everyone around me starts to leave that I realize just how long I have been sitting here.

Walking out of the prison, I feel the lowest I've felt in a long time. I have no idea what happened to Nicholas and I have no idea if he's hurt and suffering or just alone.

I have no idea if he has done something in there to lose the privilege of having a visitor.

Nicholas is not one to act out and if he did, then he was only doing it to protect himself. Still, it could be anything and not knowing makes my heart ache.

I think back to how naive my thoughts were not too long ago when it all started.

I thought that if only I was able to find out the truth then everything would fall into place.

Everyone would believe me and he would be freed immediately. Little did I know that the wheels of justice turn very slowly and it is nearly impossible for someone to convince the district attorney that they are not guilty, no matter the evidence.

I hope that's not the case with all district attorneys but, unfortunately, it seems to be the case with this one.

I don't want to go straight home and show Sydney the disappointment on my face so instead I just drive around.

It's a surprisingly warm and sunny day and I even put on a pair of sunglasses to block some of the rays.

I drive for a long time. I grab some food through the Starbucks drive-thru and then drive some more.

I don't care about being healthy anymore. I stuff my face with sugar and sweets and anything that will make my pain go away, even if it's only for a little bit.

I keep thinking about Nicholas.

Where is he?

Did he get into a fight?

Did someone hurt him?

Everything that I don't know makes me sick to my stomach. How much more of this can I take?

But what other alternative is there?

I pull the car over and park in a sprawling parking lot of some big box store and I let myself cry.

And in this moment of weakness is when I start to wonder if maybe I can't do this. I'm not strong enough to fight for someone who is behind bars and wait for them to get out.

There are many women who can do this, even for those men who have committed the crimes that they are accused and convicted of, but am I one of them?

But what's the alternative, I think to myself.

Do I just leave him there?

Do I just leave him there, knowing that

he's innocent and unable to do anything from the inside?

But what can I do on the outside?

This whole time, I thought I'd done a lot but now everything is falling apart.

Meredith has been fired for being too involved and too much on the defense's side. Luckily, they have still not found out about the preliminary DNA testing, but that makes convincing the DA's office to test the DNA that much harder. Keenan knows that Owen should be a suspect but, for some reason, he is fighting against it.

I drive home with a heavy heart. I feel stuck and out of control. I love Nicholas and I will never leave him but I also feel like everything that I'm doing has no purpose and no end.

The future seems bleak and dark and without a single hope. With the evidence they have against him now, things will only get worse.

They will take his case to trial and find him guilty. His sentence will be life without the possibility of parole.

There will be endless appeals but the chances of winning one of them are slim.

What happens to us?

Can we spend a lifetime together separated by bars?

Never speaking to each other in private?

Never holding hands?

Never touching each other?

I open the door to my apartment hoping that Sydney is not there. All I want to do is be alone right now. I want to have a cup of tea and curl up in bed and hope that this has all been a terrible dream.

"Olive," a man says when I walk into the kitchen.

Leaning against the counter, he tilts his head slightly down as his piercing eyes look deeply into mine.

My bag falls to the floor. I shake my head and cover my mouth with my hands in disbelief. He takes two steps over to me, wrapping his arms around my shoulders. My whole body starts to shake.

"Don't cry," he says, kissing my hair. "Don't cry, my sweet girl."

"What...are...you...doing here?" I mumble into his shirt.

I hold him as close as possible.

When he tries to pull away, I refuse to let him go.

"Don't go," I whisper.

"I'm not going anywhere for a long time," Nicholas says.

His arms hold me close against his chest as my hands run up and down his back feeling every part of him just to make sure that he's real.

"What are you doing here?" I ask, looking up at him.

When he presses his lips onto mine, my mouth opens and the world outside of us begins to spin. His body is hot to the touch, a perfect complement to my own cold one. He turns my head slightly to the side and kisses me harder and more passionately.

"What are you doing here?" I ask him again, through our kiss. "I went to see you today and you weren't there."

"You did? Oh, I'm so sorry."

"The guard didn't tell me anything and I thought that you got hurt again," I say. I glance up at him and suddenly see a mischievous wink. My heart skips a beat.

"What happened? How did you get out?"

I know what he's going to say before he says it. The guard didn't tell me anything because they wanted to know if I already knew.

But how?

How did he escape?

And why is he here? This is the first place they're going to look for him.

29

OLIVE

WHEN I FIND OUT...

"Okay, Olive," Nicholas says, steadying my face with his hands. I feel my eyes flickering and wildly staring at his. In return, his gaze is stoic, almost distant.

"Olive, I didn't run away," he says. His words slowly seep in.

"What happened?"

"I was released. There was a big investigation by the state of the district attorney's office for corruption and bribery. He's still in the process of stepping down since the state is trying to save face, but he's no longer working there. When Nancy reached out to the new DA and they reviewed the case against me and compared the DNA evidence they had to Owen's they found a match to both crime scenes. Nancy said that they didn't want to hold me after that."

My feet seem to crumble under me and I melt onto the floor. Nicholas kneels down to me, taking me into his arms.

"Everything is okay, Olive. I'm here with you. I'm free."

I nuzzle my head into his shoulder still unable to believe that this is real.

I feel his hands with mine and slowly move up his arms, pinching every moment to make sure that it's really him. When I get to his biceps, he flexes them, surprising me.

We both laugh and when our eyes meet again, I see a happiness in his that I haven't seen in a long time. He tilts my head up to his and brings his lips as close as possible without actually touching mine.

I feel his breath on me and inhale the sweet aroma that is his scent.

Unable to make the moment last any longer, I push myself up and kiss him.

He kisses me back almost immediately, smiling slightly against my mouth. We kiss for a long time right there on the floor. I want to take it further, but I also want to just enjoy his lips for as long as possible.

His warm breath fills my mouth and our tongues intertwine and become one. I bury my hands in his hair and he runs his up and down my shirt.

After a few minutes of making out like teenagers, he slips his hand under my shirt. I straighten my back and kiss him harder. He reciprocates by gently lowering me onto the hardwood floor and draping his body over mine.

"I missed this," I whisper.

"Me, too."

We stay in the moment for a long time. Kissing and not kissing, more like nuzzling and just enjoying being with one another.

But after a little bit, the clothes that separate us start to get in the way. We discard them quickly and move to the bed.

He lies down on the sheets next to me and looks at my breasts. He runs his fingers up and down the outline of my curves and I revel in his six pack and his wide, broad shoulders.

He laughs when I pinch his butt and then

climbs on top of me and flexes it when I grab it harder.

He grabs my thighs and opens them up.

He wraps them around his hips and I arch my back and pull him inside of me.

He looks at me for a long time and then kisses me again. His kiss is slow and moves in sync with his hips.

With each thrust, my body seems to open up a little more and welcome him in a little further. I run my hands up his back and dig my fingers into his flesh when I feel myself getting close.

He looks at me for a moment and I wait for him to say, "Tell me to stop," those words that have echoed in my mind ever since the first time he had ever spoken them to me.

But he doesn't.

Instead, he puts his lips on mine and moans my name.

My body suddenly fills with fire. It's so hot, I feel like I'm surrounded by flames. He thrusts again and again and the temperature only increases. He whispers my name over and over again.

I flip him over and climb on top of him. I

press my hands into his chest and arch my back as I sit on top of him. Now, I can feel his full girth as I start to move my thighs up and down.

"I love you," he whispers.

"I love you, too," I say, tilting my head and letting my hair fall down my back.

He runs his hands up and down my stomach, cupping my breasts and eventually pulling me closer to him.

A warm sensation starts to build in my core. It's familiar of course, but this time, it overwhelms me.

Taking me completely by surprise, I yell out his name and collapse on top of him in a state of euphoria and contentment.

LATER THAT EVENING, after we get dressed, there's a knock on the door. I think that it's probably Sydney and she might have forgotten her keys but it's actually Meredith.

"I knew your address and one of your neighbors was walking out so she let me in," she says.

"We've got quite a secure building here," I joke. She laughs. I invite her in and introduce her to Nicholas.

She extends her hand but instead of shaking it, he comes right over and gives her a big warm hug.

"Thank you so much for everything you have done for me. Olive told me all about it and I wouldn't be here without you."

"You're welcome," she says shyly. "I was just so drawn to your story right from the beginning and the more I started investigating the more I knew I had to do the right thing."

We order takeout and while we wait, Meredith tells us all about what has been happening back at the office.

"I knew that something was going on with Keenan starting about two years ago," she says. "He used to really care about his job but then he got distracted and absentminded. At first, we at the office all thought that he was just going through a midlife crisis or having an affair or both but then I heard rumors that he was in a lot of financial trouble. He owed debts to a lot of bad people around town. The worst of the worst, as you can imagine."

I nod and urge her to continue.

"Is that why he wanted to frame me for what happened to David and Nina?" Nicholas asks.

"I don't think the corruption and the bribery necessarily had to do with that. I know that when it came to you, he was set in his ways. He just believed that you did it and that was it. That's one of the reasons he refused to test the DNA. He didn't want to have proof of something to the contrary."

"So, what happened?" I ask.

"We, at the office, mainly me but another paralegal as well, we started gathering evidence secretly. Just anything that we found suspicious. And when we thought we had a good case, we turned that over to the authorities. He suspected something because that's when he fired me."

I shake my head. "I thought that he fired you because he found out that we tested the DNA."

"No." She smiles. "I wouldn't have gotten my job back if that were the case. Luckily, no one knows about that and hopefully no one ever will."

"So, what's going to happen now?" Nicholas asks.

"The new DA is working on the case against Owen. He gave Robert immunity in exchange for his testimony and I think he's working on the same deal for Ricky."

"Wow, that's great," I say.

"They are going to officially serve him the papers and arrest him at the jail tomorrow," Meredith says. "He's already incarcerated so the two states will have to work out some sort of arrangement. I guess he'll first stand trial for what he did to you, Olive, and then be extradited here to face the murder charges."

A feeling of euphoria mixed with relief sweeps over my whole body and I finally relax.

Owen will finally get what is coming to him. He will finally get what he deserves.

30

OLIVE

WHEN WE PREPARE FOR HER WEDDING...

After Nicholas' release, we spend every waking moment together and we still can't get enough of each other.

We sleep in late.

We go to lunch and then spend our afternoons in bed.

We laugh and talk and lose ourselves in each other and it's never enough.

We go to the movies and eat dinner and sleep in each other's arms. He lives in my room and Sydney doesn't seem to mind. James wasn't able to get a job in Boston but did get one in New York and they plan on moving there after they get married.

At first, her pregnancy doesn't seem very

difficult but then the exhaustion sets in. So, she has been spending most of her days planning the wedding and taking long naps.

I keep meaning to talk to her about marrying him again, but every time I see them, they actually look happy.

When I talk about it to Nicholas, he doesn't offer much advice outside of saying that some people can get over infidelity and maybe even learn to be happy in the future especially now that they're having a baby.

I want to argue with him but in reality, I don't know if my arguments are right.

Deep in my heart, I know that she deserves someone who will love every part of her the way that Nicholas loves me and I don't see that in James. But given everything else that's going on, the baby and her mother cutting her out of her inheritance if she breaks up with him, maybe Sydney is doing what's right for her.

With James away in New York, working crazy hours, Sydney mainly stays in her room. Tonight, I insist on her joining us for dinner and a movie. Reluctantly, she agrees.

"I don't want to be some third wheel," she

says, carrying her blanket from her bed to the couch.

"Well, first of all, you're not a third wheel, there's two of you in there," I joke.

This makes her laugh and snuggle into the couch. Nicholas brings us both tea and sits down next to me, draping his arm over my shoulder.

"You two are so cute," she says.

Her tone is casual but there's a sadness in her eyes. I want to ask her about it but it doesn't feel like she wants to talk about it.

"So, how's everything going for the wedding?" Nicholas asks. "Is there anything else we can do?"

Sydney shrugs and just stares at the screen as the Netflix logo loads. "No, not really. There isn't even much for me to do. Mom's taking care of everything."

And that's exactly what she means. Her mother has picked out the flowers, arranged for the venue, and chosen the band.

Her mother made all of the catering arrangements including the kind of signature drink they will have and the look and the filling of the wedding cake.

At first, Sydney seemed to resist all of this but after a bit, she just gave up and ignored that it was happening.

"Agh!" Sydney yells out in pain. Her face contorts as she tries to breathe but she can't.

"Oh, no!" she yelps, grabbing her stomach. "Something's wrong...agh!"

"We have to get her to the hospital now," Nicholas says, standing up.

"No hospital," Sydney says. "No, I can't go to the hospital....agh!" She bends in half, cradling her stomach.

"Syd, something is wrong. Something might be happening to the baby we have to get you help."

She continues to refuse, insisting that everything is fine while we get her into the car and Nicholas rushes to the hospital.

He drops us off at the emergency entrance and I help her inside. A nurse quickly puts her into a wheelchair and takes her away.

It takes me almost forty minutes to fill out all of Sydney's paperwork. Mainly, because I don't know a lot of the answers, especially when it comes to her family's medical history, but also because I can't focus on any of it at this moment. My thoughts keep going back to her and what is going on with her baby.

I hold Nicholas' hand and hope more than anything that both she and the baby are going to be fine. I keep trying James's number and leave him five messages but he still doesn't reply. But when Nicholas tries, he answers.

"He's actually in Boston," Nicholas says, hanging up. "He'll be here soon."

"What do you mean he's in Boston? Isn't he working at his new job in New York? Sydney said that he has crazy hours there."

Nicholas doesn't meet my eyes and instead just looks down.

"He's cheating on her again, isn't he?" I ask.

He doesn't respond. He doesn't have to. I am pretty certain that he is.

Nicholas takes my hand into his. "I'm sorry he's such an asshole," he whispers. "I had no idea he was really like this. I wish I had never introduced them."

"Me, too," I whisper. Except that's not

really true. Without them meeting, then we would've never met either.

Hours pass. Sydney's mom comes by but doesn't stay. She says that she has an event that she can't miss but will be by later. It's a shitty thing to do but I'm glad that I don't have to make small talk with her in the waiting room.

"Where is he?" I turn to Nicholas. "Have you heard anything?"

He shakes his head and dials his number again. When Nicholas gets up and takes the call privately, a doctor walks up to me.

He asks if I'm the next of kin. I tell him that she's my best friend and roommate and her mother isn't here.

"Good," the doctor says, smiling slightly. "She told me that under no circumstances does she want to see her."

I nod and furrow my brow, not sure what is going on.

He shows me to her room and I motion to Nicholas to come over after he's done. In the middle of the room, I see her sitting up in the adjustable bed. Her face is almost without color but there's a smile on her face. I let out a small sigh of relief.

"You are one lucky girl," the doctor says. "If you didn't get here when you did, you would've lost the baby."

She nods and looks at Nicholas with tears in her eyes.

———

SHE STAYS in the hospital overnight and I curl up on the chair next to her. James never comes over and neither does her mother. I tell Nicholas to go home but he stays and sleeps out in the waiting room. When the nurses wake Sydney up with a breakfast tray, and I take a sip of her coffee, she tells me that she has made a decision.

"I'm not getting married."

"What do you mean? Your wedding is in five days."

She shrugs.

"What about everything you said?"

"What happened last night was everything that I needed to know about both my mother and James. I needed them, but they were nowhere to be found."

I'm about to say something but it's hard to argue with the truth.

"I don't need them in my life especially if having them means only existing on their terms."

I give her a sight nod. I want to believe her but I'm afraid that she's just saying this now and will go ahead and marry James anyway.

"I heard what you and Nicholas were saying last night," she adds, her voice cracking.

My throat closes up.

Oh, no, she was supposed to be asleep.

"I wasn't," she says, reading my mind. "He was in New York, huh? He was in Boston and when Nicholas told him what happened to me, he went to a strip club instead."

A part of me wishes that we had talked about this out in the waiting room, but now I know that it's right for her to know the truth, however she found out about it.

"My baby and I deserve better," Sydney

says. "I'm going to take care of her on my own."

"Her?" My eyes light up. She laughs and nods.

"Yep, they told me the sex. It's a girl."

I wrap my arms around her. "I'm so happy for you, Sydney. Now I get to be an auntie!"

"You're going to be the best auntie in the world!"

"I'll always be here for you," I whisper into her ear and hold her for a long time.

31

NICHOLAS

WHEN I INVITE HER TO DINNER...

Sometimes, you have to go through a whole lot of shit to realize how lucky you really are.

These last few weeks with Olive have changed my life. I thought that I loved her before but now my love has magnified.

Being with her in a real place and being a normal couple, without the drama of what our lives were like before, has made me realize exactly why I want to spend the rest of my life with her.

Real life is all about the everyday moments. You can have an explosive love that takes you from one day to another, but it's the moments in between that matter the most.

The person to marry is the one who you want to sit on the couch with forever.

It's the person who can make you laugh and fill your heart with excitement and happiness.

It's the person you want to go on an adventure with, life being the biggest adventure ever.

I invite her to dinner to our favorite restaurant. It's modern and elegant but not particularly upscale.

It's comfortable and it's the place we have gone to a number of times since I got released. Originally, I planned on waiting until dessert but I'm too nervous to prolong this much longer.

As soon as the server brings us our drinks, I get down on one knee and look into her beautiful wide eyes.

"Olive Kernes, I have loved you since the moment I met you. And that's a difficult thing for me to admit since I don't believe in love at first sight."

She lets out a small laugh but her body continues to tremble.

"Olive Kernes, will you make me the happiest man in the world and marry me?"

I open the ring box and look up at her. She doesn't even look at the ring, and instead just stares into my eyes. Big fat tears roll down her cheeks. She covers her mouth with her hand and nods.

"Is that a yes?" I ask, also tearing up.

"Yes," she manages through the sobs. "Yes, a million times yes."

Our food arrives when we are still wiping away the last of our tears. People around us clap and celebrate with us and the server brings us a complimentary bottle of champagne.

"What kind of wedding do you think you want?" I ask, taking a bite of my salad. She doesn't answer right away, instead locking her eyes on the diamond ring on her left hand.

"This isn't real, right?" she asks after a moment.

I shrug.

"C'mon, this must be three carats or something ridiculous." She laughs.

"Something ridiculous," I say coyly.

"Did you seriously spend all of your money on this ring? 'Cause if you did then you're in serious trouble."

I laugh again, but she kicks me under the table until I stop.

"Let me level with you," I say, taking a sip of the champagne. "It is three and a half carats, with the highest quality diamond and a platinum band."

Olive shakes her head in disbelief.

"But I did not spend all of my money on it. Actually, if you want to be technical, it's our money, remember? The Monet was actually worth a lot more than we thought and I was able to fetch a cool ten for it."

"Ten? Ten what?"

I tilt my head without saying a word.

"Ten million?" she asks, whispering the word million while looking around the room hoping that no one is eavesdropping on our conversation. I give her a slight nod.

"Are you serious?"

I give her another nod.

"But...how?" she asks. "Owen didn't tell me where he hid it and he wasn't going to tell you."

"Of course not." I laugh. "But he's also a creature of habit. He didn't know many people on the outside he could trust and he certainly couldn't put it in a safe deposit box so he hid it in the only place he knew of."

"Where?" Olive asks.

"Your mom's house."

"Really?" she asks, spitting out her crouton. "Are you serious?"

I shrug and flash her a smile.

"Oh my God, I was such an idiot for not checking there."

"Eh, it was just a fluke that it was there," I say generously. "I figured it was worth a look and it turned out that it was more than worth it."

"How did you do it?" Olive asks, grabbing a piece of French bread and breaking it in half.

"Same way I've always done it," I say with a shrug. "I snuck in once to see if it was there, took pictures, made a replica, and then snuck in again and switched it."

Olive starts to laugh. "Owen is going to be so mad," she says. "Honestly, I'm a little surprised that my mom hasn't sold it."

"I don't think she knew that it was real. I think she's keeping it for sentimental reasons."

"Well, in that case, she should be perfectly happy with the fake one," she says, pulling my hand to her lips and kissing it.

"You never answered my question," I point out when our dessert arrives.

"What's that?"

"What kind of wedding do you want?"

32

OLIVE

WHEN WE EXCHANGE VOWS...

We drive to the courthouse together two days later. I'm dressed in jeans and a white knit top. Instead of satin heels, I wear mid-calf vegan leather boots.

The day is dreary and cold but I feel anything but that in my heart and mind. I am about to marry my best friend and the love of my life and I know that no matter what happens in the future my love for him and his love for me is never going to change.

I didn't want to wear a gown or even a dress and even though it's eating Sydney up on the inside, she bites her tongue and lets me do what I want to.

I know that this day is supposed to be

special and we make it special by dressing up but in my case, I'd rather just wear what I feel comfortable in, knowing that it's going to be special no matter what.

As I walk into the judge's chambers, I don't feel any regrets about anything. When my eyes meet Nicholas' and he gives me that wink of his, I know that we are going to be happy for a very long time.

"I, Nicholas, take you, Olive, to be my friend, my lover, and my wife. I will be yours in times of plenty and in times of want, in times of sickness and in times of health, in times of joy and in times of sorrow, in times of failure and in times of triumph."

Tears start to stream down my face as my body trembles. His voice cracks a little as he continues, "I promise to cherish and respect you, to care for and protect you, to comfort and encourage you, and to stay with you for all eternity."

I take a deep breath. Now, it's my turn.

"I, Olive, take you, Nicholas, to be my husband, my partner, and my one true love. I will cherish and love you for the rest of my days. I will trust and respect you, laugh with you and cry with you and love you through good times and bad."

"Nicholas, do you take this woman to be your wife?" the judge asks.

"I do," he whispers, squeezing my hand.

"Olive, do you take this man to be your husband?"

"Of course," I mumble through the tears. I hear their laughter behind me.

"You're supposed to say, 'I do,' honey," Josephine says. She flew in on the red-eye last night just to be here for this moment.

"Let's try this again," the judge suggests and asks me again.

I look into his eyes and smile.

"I do," I say and we put on our wedding rings.

"By the power vested in me by the State of Massachusetts, I now pronounce you husband and wife. You may now kiss."

Nicholas takes me into his arms and presses his lips onto mine.

A YEAR AND A HALF LATER...

LYING on my back in the cool refreshing water, I watch him from a distance. The waves aren't very big today but Nicholas is still out there on his surfboard giving it his all. He looks just as muscular and sexy as ever and with that sun-kissed tan, he looks even more gorgeous.

I watch the turquoise water run over my fingers as I dip them below the horizon and taste its saltiness with my tongue.

Going swimming has become something of a mid-morning ritual for us over the past year and we even schedule our plans to make sure that we don't miss it. This morning, however, I have to cut the swimming short.

"You're going in already?" Nicholas yells, getting up after riding another wave.

"Yeah, I have some work to do," I say, waddling out onto the shore. The weightlessness that I felt disappears and I'm suddenly reminded of exactly how heavy I really am. One more month to go, I say to myself, rubbing my giant belly.

I walk down the sandy pathway leading

up to our cottage. A nearby palm tree sways in the light breeze. I open the gate to the white-picket fence and glance at the freshly painted blue shutters.

Inside, I place the laptop on the dining room table right next to the window overlooking the ocean and watch Nicholas go after another wave.

I open the computer and scroll through the five chapters that I have already written. Mom, who I used to call Josephine, gave me the idea and it is to her that this book, the story of how we fell in love, is dedicated.

I look over my notes of what I want to cover in the next chapter and begin to write.

***

Thank you for reading TELL ME TO LIE!

I hope you enjoyed the epic conclusion of Nicholas and Olive's story. Want to dig into another AMAZING novel?

One-click DANGEROUS ENGAGEMENT now!

Not long ago, there was nothing I couldn't

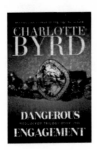

have. Now, I don't even have the choice of whom to marry.

To save my father's life and our family's legacy, I have to marry a cruel man who wants me only as a trophy.

Henry Asher was just supposed to be a summer fling, but we fell in love. We thought we would be together forever, but life got in the way. After we broke up, I vowed to never tell Henry the truth about my engagement.

What happens when the lies that were supposed to save me start to drown me?

HENRY ASHER

I didn't always have wealth or power. There was even a time when I didn't want any of that.

Then I met her: Aurora Tate is an heiress to a billion-dollar fortune. She grew up on Park Avenue, had a house in the Hamptons and skied in Aspen. Our first summer together was magical. We were naive enough to think that love was going to be enough.

Now, she's forced to marry a man she hates to save her father's life.

To get her back and to make her my wife, I need to become the man she needs me to be.

Can I do it in time?

One-click DANGEROUS ENGAGEMENT now!

I APPRECIATE you sharing my books and telling your friends about them. Reviews help readers find my books! Please leave a review on your favorite site.

Turn the page to read an excerpt of Dangerous Engagement (Wedlock Trilogy Book 1)!

EXCERPT OF DANGEROUS ENGAGEMENT (WEDLOCK TRILOGY BOOK 1)

C hapter 1 - Aurora

I watch him from afar. I know him even though I don't even know his name. He probably wants everything that's mine. He imagines that my life is wonderful and fun and full of possibilities that he could only dream of. What he doesn't know is how boring it can be or how isolating.

I have my parents, my friends, my parents extended social circle, and even my grandparents. But none of them really know me. I wish they did.

Not even my therapist knows me.

Everywhere I go, I wear a false face and it makes my life a farce.

My makeup and dress are my armor.

Thousand dollar shoes. Two thousand dollar bags. Three thousand dollar dresses.

My closet is as big as most one-bedroom apartments in New York City. I can buy anything and therefore, I want nothing.

My therapist thinks that I'm depressed. She diagnosed me with anxiety and post-traumatic stress disorder and prescribed meds that I don't want to take. Maybe I am depressed. But who wouldn't be? I'm in my mid-twenties and I can be anything I want. The only problem is that I don't want to do anything.

During the year I stay busy by going to school. The classes give me some structure to the day.

I take four each semester and between that, studying, the gym, and the weekly spa session, I manage to stay busy enough to forget how bored I am.

On the weekends, my girlfriends, the ones working sixty hours a week at non-paying internships for famous designers, artists, and gallery owners insist that I pull myself away from my books and my boring grad-school "friends" and hang with them instead. Their parties are usually two-day affairs that require helicopter rides and mansions in far-flung places. It's the stuff of dreams, or in my case, nightmares.

They say *friends* using quotation marks because they know that those people are not really my friends at all. They're just people I know. What my other friends don't know, however, is that they aren't really my friends either. They are just people I have known longer.

This guy with his hazel eyes, casual smile, and cheap clothes probably thinks the same thing of me as everyone else. That I'm just a spoiled little girl who has had everything handed to her, that I have never worked hard for anything, and I will never deserve anything I have.

I don't blame him. A part of me thinks the same way. What else can you think? My father owns a media empire and has dominated New York society ever since he came onto the scene in the 1980s. He owns hundreds of buildings and homes in New York and around the world. He's someone every businessman wants to be but can't because he will never step down.

I'm his oldest child and he wants to groom me to take over, but I know that that will never happen. He is not the type to retire. He's not the type to fade away. Besides, I have no interest in running an empire. I want to carve out my own place in this world, what that is exactly I do not know yet.

Neither of my parents understand this, even though they should. They both came from nothing and they both grew Tate Media into what it is today. My mother was not the type to stay at home. She is Tate's Chief Financial Officer and that's just scratching the surface of what she does there.

My parents are Tate Media. They have built it from scratch, buying up one distressed radio station at a time. They know the ins and outs of the whole business and, despite all of that, they have never made me feel welcome there.

I have spent one long and miserable summer there during my sophomore year with both of them looking over my shoulder and micro-managing my every move. After that, I said no more and promised myself that I would never work there again.

The guy glances at me. I sit back in the lounger and point my toes. I take a sip of my margarita, pursing my lips just so. I adjust my Chanel sunglasses and oversized floppy hat to both hide my gaze and to get a better look at him.

He's cute enough and probably witty, to a degree, but I wish that people weren't so predictable. I know exactly what he's going to say before he says it. I know exactly what he's going to compliment me on and what he's going to pay attention to. There is no surprise and without that, he will be just like a hundred others I've met who did not hold my interest.

He walks up to me slowly. I brace myself for a boring pick-up line. He looks deep into my eyes, so deeply in fact that I can't look away. I pull my sunglasses to the bridge of my nose and wait for him to open his mouth. His lips curl at the corners, but only slightly.

"Have you ever read Flannery O'Connor?"

I sit back in my seat, taken aback. Hmm... this is interesting.

"Of course," I say, raising one eyebrow.

"She's one of my favorite writers," he says, spreading his shoulders out widely. He holds a mop in one hand and with the other runs his fingers through his hair.

The confidence he exudes is overwhelming, and a little off-putting. "Why are you asking about her?"

"Well, I was just reading one of her stories this morning before work, *Good Country People*. You know it?"

I nod.

"Really?" he asks as if he doesn't believe me.

He is challenging me, which is not something that usually happens. No, let me amend that. That's not something that has *ever* happened.

"It's about Joy, a thirty-two-year-old atheist and a PhD student of philosophy who lives with her small-minded mother," I say, focusing my eyes directly on his. "Joy doesn't have a leg because she lost it in a childhood shooting accident. A Bible salesman comes to see them and her mother believes that he is good country people, as they say. Then he invites Joy out for a date and that's when things get, let's just say interesting."

He raises his eyebrows and takes a step away from me.

"Are you surprised?" I ask.

"Yes, to tell you the truth I am. Pleasantly."

"Why is that?" I ask.

"It's pretty obscure," he says with a pronounced shrug.

I fold my arms across my chest and raise my chin in the air in defiance.

"Did you bring it up to teach me a lesson?" I ask. "Maybe make me feel bad, or stupid even?"

He shakes his head. When I look into his eyes, I can't look away. There's something in them that pulls me in, even convincing me that he didn't mean it that way at all. It was a genuine attempt to make a connection.

"While they are on their date, the Bible salesman persuades her to go up in the loft and to take off her prosthetic leg," he says. His words come out smoothly, naturally even. "He then shows her the inside of one of his Bibles that contains a bottle of whiskey, condoms, and cards with naked women on them."

"When she says no to his advance," I finish the story for him, "the Bible salesman tells her that he collects fake legs and takes off with hers."

"What do you like about the story?" he asks.

"Who said that I liked it?" I ask him.

He smiles.

"You have to."

"I have to?" I ask.

"You know it so intimately and innately that they must've made an imprint on your soul," he says.

I gaze into his eyes. I have lived for twenty-five years and not once have I ever spoken with another human being about the existence of a soul. Yet here is a stranger, a simple worker on my father's yacht, who speaks of it as if it's second nature, as if it's as real as gravity.

"I think what I like about it, and what I like about Flannery O'Connor's work in general is her sense of irony," I say. "It's comedic. The title of the story is *Good Country People*, and that's exactly what her mother thinks the Bible salesman is. And yet he is the furthest thing from that. And even she, with her advanced degree, is someone who should know better, but she doesn't. It's almost funny. But then again, my own mother thinks I have a perverse sense of humor."

"I think we might have that in common," he says.

Our voices die down and all we are left with is a sweet silence that is both comforting and comfortable. I want to stay in this moment forever but we are quickly interrupted.

"Hey, you missed one hell of a lunch! Did you get some of that alone time you wanted?" Ellis Holte asks. She plops down on the lounger next to me and asks the guy who I've been talking to for a refill of her drink.

"No, he doesn't do that," I interject. But he just shrugs his shoulders and says he will get it for her anyway.

"Are you seriously at this point, already?" she asks.

"What are you talking about?"

"You know what I'm talking about," she says, pointing to her index finger adorned with a three-carat diamond ring in my face. It's not an engagement ring, it's a *just because* ring. "Are you already messing around with the *help*? I thought we would only be doing that when we are seven years into boring marriages, not while we are still single."

"I'm not messing around with anyone," I say sternly.

I don't even know his name I note to myself. I run my tongue over my lower lip and repress the desire to talk to him again. Why do I even care?

Why am I so interested all of a sudden?

He is one of the only people that, no correct that, he is *the* only person who I have met who hasn't bored me. I couldn't predict anything that was going to come out of his mouth and I want more of that.

Unfortunately, I don't see him again until later that night. His boss is watching his every move to make sure that he is doing a good job cleaning all of the decks of my father's boat. Of course, I could go up and talk to him myself, but I'm not quite ready to go that far out of my comfort zone.

After spending the whole day drinking, talking, and reading magazines, the girls are ready to shower, do their hair, and go out for a night on the town. Begrudgingly, I go through the motions as well. I finish before the rest and take a circle around the yacht, hoping to run into him again.

Him. The guy whose name I don't even know.

Though I don't see him, I do see the manager. Mr. Madsen is in his sixties and has worked on my father's boat, overseeing all personnel, for as long as I can remember.

"Mr. Madsen, do you happen to know where I can find the guy who was cleaning the decks earlier today?" I ask as casually as possible.

If he wants to give me a knowing smile, he doesn't. Mr. Madsen is the epitome of professionalism.

"We had a few people working that position today. Henry Asher, Tom Cedar, and Elliot Dickinson."

"Um, he was about six feet tall with broad shoulders and thick dark hair."

"Oh, yes, you're referring to Henry Asher. He is probably downstairs in the crew quarters."

"Thank you very much," I say, going straight to the staircase.

Appalled, Mr. Madsen rushes over to me and blocks my way.

"I will, of course, get him to come upstairs to see you, Miss Tate," he says quickly. "If you don't mind waiting in the living room."

I don't really want to wait, but I decide to go along with it. The guests are not supposed to go down to the crew quarters. It has been that way since the beginning of time. Besides, I don't really want my friends to see me going down there anyway.

Before I have the chance to glance at my watch for the second time in five minutes, he appears in the doorway. He looks just as tall, dark, and handsome as he did earlier today, only this time the angles in his face and his muscles look even more defined as a result of the tan settling deeper into his skin.

"Hi," he says, hanging his head just a little, before turning his eyes up to mine.

"Hi," I say quietly.

"You wanted to see me?" His hair falls slightly into his face as he leans on the side of the wall like some sort of modern day James Dean.

What the hell do I say now? This is the first time I have ever even made an inkling of a first move on a guy. It feels foreign and unnatural and yet exciting at the same time.

"I was just wondering," I say slowly, "if you wanted to join me ashore tonight?"

He raises his eyebrows before smiling out of the corner of his mouth.

"Of course," he says confidently. "What did you have in mind?"

"Well, I was going to go out with my girlfriends. We'll probably go dancing or something like that. Nothing is set in stone."

Henry takes a few steps closer and sits down on the couch right next to me. I turn my body toward his so that our knees are nearly touching.

"Well, if it's not set in stone," he says, "what do you think about doing something else instead?"

"Like what?"

"How about dinner at one of my favorite taco stands? Followed by a few drinks at a shitty but incredibly fun dive bar?"

Anyone else in his position would try to impress me by taking me to some fancy five-star restaurant and fumble through the wine list. Anyone else would try to pretend that they were a lot more worldly than he is, even though we both know that he works crew on my father's boat.

But he doesn't.

I am intrigued and surprised by his audacity. He is a breath of fresh air that's so intoxicating, it leaves me disoriented.

One-click DANGEROUS ENGAGEMENT now!

CONNECT WITH CHARLOTTE BYRD

Sign up for my **newsletter** to find out when I have new books!

You can also join my Facebook group, **Charlotte Byrd's Reader Club**, for exclusive giveaways and sneak peaks of future books.

I appreciate you sharing my books and telling your friends about them. Reviews help readers find my books! Please leave a review on your favorite site.

Want to hear about new releases, free books and get exclusive giveaways?

Sign up for my newsletter!

ALSO BY CHARLOTTE BYRD

All books are available at ALL major retailers! If you can't find it, please email me at charlotte@charlotte-byrd.com

Wedlocked Trilogy
Dangerous Engagement
Lethal Wedding
Fatal Wedding

Tell me Series
Tell Me to Stop
Tell Me to Go
Tell Me to Stay
Tell Me to Run
Tell Me to Fight

Tell Me to Lie

Tangled Series
Tangled up in Ice
Tangled up in Pain
Tangled up in Lace
Tangled up in Hate
Tangled up in Love

Black Series
Black Edge
Black Rules
Black Bounds
Black Contract
Black Limit

Lavish Trilogy
Lavish Lies
Lavish Betrayal
Lavish Obsession

Standalone Novels
Debt
Offer
Unknown
Dressing Mr. Dalton

ABOUT CHARLOTTE BYRD

Charlotte Byrd is the bestselling author of many contemporary romance novels. She lives in Southern California with her husband, son, and a crazy toy Australian Shepherd. She loves books, hot weather and crystal blue waters.

Write her here:

charlotte@charlotte-byrd.com

Check out her books here:

www.charlotte-byrd.com

Connect with her here:

www.facebook.com/charlottebyrdbooks

www.instagram.com/charlottebyrdbooks

www.twitter.com/byrdauthor

Want to hear about new releases, free books and get exclusive giveaways?

Sign up for my newsletter!

YOU ARE INVITED!
Want to hear about new releases, free books and get exclusive
giveaways?
Join my Facebook Group!

facebook.com/charlottebyrdbooks

twitter.com/byrdauthor

instagram.com/charlottebyrdbooks

bookbub.com/profile/charlotte-byrd

Made in United States
North Haven, CT
06 September 2024

57065406R00181